PARADISE

Other Graphia Titles

The Road to Damietta
by Scott O'Dell

The Fattening Hut
by Pat Lowery Collins

A Certain Slant of Light
by Laura Whitcomb

Owl in Love
by Patrice Kindl

Story for a Black Night
by Clayton Bess

Zazoo
by Richard Mosher

Lost in the Labyrinth
by Patrice Kindl

Real Time
by Pnina Moed Kass

I Just Hope It's Lethal: Poems of Sadness, Madness, and Joy
edited by Liz Rosenberg and Deena November

PARADISE

Inspired by a True Story of Survival

JOAN ELIZABETH GOODMAN

An Imprint of Houghton Mifflin Company
BOSTON

*To friendship—the magnification of my heart—
transcending time, distance, and even death*

Published in the United States by Graphia, an imprint of
Houghton Mifflin Company, Boston, Massachusetts.
Originally published in hardcover in the United States by
Houghton Mifflin Company, Boston, in 2002.
Graphia and the Graphia logo are registered trademarks of Houghton Mifflin Company.

www.houghtonmifflinbooks.com

The text of this book is set in 12-point Dante.
Maps illustrated by the author.

Library of Congress Cataloging-in-Publication Data
Goodman, Joan E.
Paradise / by Joan Elizabeth Goodman.
p. cm.
Summary: In 1542, eager to escape the French Huguenot household
of her harsh father, sixteen-year-old Marguerite de La Rocque sails
with her equally stern uncle, the Sieur de Roberval, to the New World,
where she is left alone on an island with only her young Catholic
lover and her chaperone to help her survive.
PAP ISBN 0-618-49481-2   ISBN 0-618-11450-5
1. Canada—History—To 1763 (New France)—Juvenile fiction. [1. Canada—
History—To 1763 (New France) —Fiction. 2. Survival—Fiction.] I. Title.
PZ7.G61375 Par 2002   [Fic]—dc21   2001051918

HC ISBN-13 978-0618-11450-4
PAP ISBN-13 978-0618-49481-1

Manufactured in the United States of America
HAD 10 9 8 7 6 5 4 3 2 1

GLOSSARY

adieu goodbye

aionnesta stag (Native American)⋆

argent silver, money

Basque native of the western Pyrenees on the Bay of Biscay in Spain

bien good ("eh bien!": well!)

Bon Dieu Good Lord (God)

bonjour good day

bon voyage have a pleasant journey

Breton native of Bretagne (Brittany), on the north coast of France

cabane, la the cabin

cacacomy bread (Native American)⋆

canu canoe (Native American)⋆

château (*pl.* châteaux) mansion

courage courage, have courage

d'accord agreed

d'Arry the estate of Pierre's family

Demoiselle young lady

de rien it is nothing

harquebus heavy gun invented in the fifteenth century

livres pounds (monetary units)

ma chérie my darling

Madame Madam, Mrs.

Mademoiselle Miss

mais, oui but, yes

Maison, La The House

Maman Mama

ma mère my mother

ma petite my little one

merci thank you

Mon Dieu My God

Mont Blanc White Mountain, the highest peak in the Alps

Montron the estate of the de La Rocques, consisting of the great house, fields, woods, orchards, and village of those who served the family

orlop the lowest deck on a ship

pas mal not bad

Saguenay the mythical kingdom described to Cartier by the Huron chief, Donnaconna. He claimed that Saguenay was rich in jewels and spices, and inhabited by winged men who flew about like bats. Cartier thought he'd found gold, thus supporting Donnaconna's tale. It turned out to be "fools' gold"—iron pyrite.

Saint-Jean Saint John—the bay and settlement on Newfoundland

Saint-Laurent Saint Lawrence—the gulf and river of eastern Canada

sauvages, les the wild men ("ma petite sauvage": my little wild child)

Sieur Lord—only nobility might use this title, unlike the more modern *Monsieur* or *Mister*

s'il vous plait if you please

sou penny

Terre-Neuve Newfoundland— discovered by John Cabot, sailing for England in 1497. Soon after European fisherman went there to harvest the plentiful cod.

triste sad

tu comprends? do you understand?

Vôtre Majesté Your Majesty

⋆Native terms are from "The Three Voyages of Cartier" in *Early English and French Voyages, 1534–1608,* Henry S. Burrage. These natives may have been Iroquois from the St. Lawrence Valley, or Beothuk from Newfoundland. Cartier referred to them only as *les sauvages.*

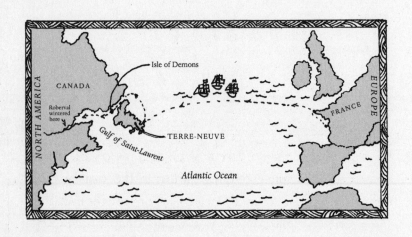

PREFACE

In 1536 all of france marveled over the adventures of Captain Jacques Cartier in the vast land of Canada, across the Atlantic Ocean. Cartier brought back the native chief Donnaconna, who told the king of a country inhabited by white men, called Saguenay. He said gold, emeralds, and diamonds were there, at the end of a river, deep in the Canadian wilderness.

Plans went quickly forward to colonize Canada and mine its wealth. Jean-François de La Rocque, the Sieur de Roberval, was appointed lieutenant general in charge of the expedition. Among the first Frenchwomen he brought to the Canadian wilderness was his niece Marguerite de La Rocque. This novel is based on her true story.

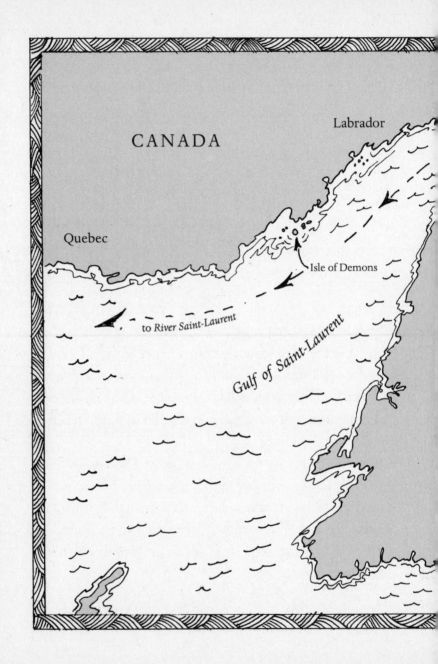

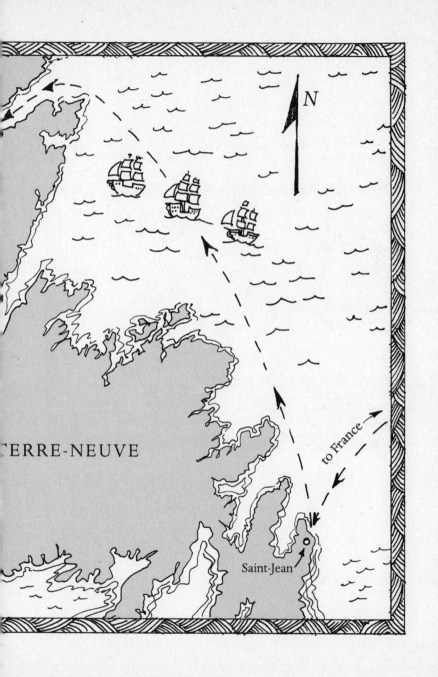

N

TERRE-NEUVE

to France

Saint-Jean

ISLE OF DEMONS

It began with such promise. We would create a new Eden.
Who could have guessed how it would end?

ONE

LITTLE ISABEAU AND I HUDDLED BY THE KITCHEN hearth, the only fire allowed in Montron after February, when Father had declared that winter was over and we no longer needed fires. I was teaching my sister how to hem a bed sheet, just as Maman had once taught me. The child looked weary. We both needed a rest. Since Maman's death of a wasting sickness last year ours had been an unending round of tasks with little chance of escape. I stood up and stretched, letting my work fall to the floor. Isabeau looked up, startled.

"Come along," I said. "Let's go to the pantry and beg Cook for bread and honey."

"Marguerite! We mustn't. Father said—"

"Yes, I know, but Father cannot begrudge us a crust of bread." Although we both knew well that he did.

Damienne came rushing into the room.

"Your father wants you immediately in his study," she said, her face red with excitement.

"Whatever for?"

"And why should Sieur de La Rocque tell a serving wench his intentions?" said Damienne.

"You know something," I said. "And I shall tickle it out of you."

"Mademoiselle Marguerite, I know nothing, only that you must hurry."

"Will Father punish Marguerite?" asked Isabeau, tears already pooling in her blue eyes.

"No, *ma chérie*," said Damienne. "Your father was smiling."

Smiling! Dear Lord, Father didn't smile. What could it be?

Damienne helped me pull off my apron and tidy my hair. She scooped up Isabeau, and we raced through the gray stone halls of Montron, across the cheerless court, to the heavy oak door of Father's study. I caught my breath and tried to assume the quiet, joyless manner that Father expected of me. I knocked.

Albert, my younger brother, opened the door. My older brothers, Marcel and fat Christophe, stood at attention before Father's wide table. Their faces showed only impatience. This was very strange. It looked as if my brothers knew as little of my father's plans as I did. Absorbed in his accounts, as always, Father seemed unaware of my entrance.

I went to where my brothers stood and curtsied to the

ground. I kept away from Marcel, who was apt to kick me if he thought he could get away with it. Damienne and Isabeau knew enough to remain behind in the shadows.

"Marguerite!"

My father spoke and I rose to my feet.

"Yes, sire."

"Your uncle, Jean-François de La Rocque, Sieur de Roberval, has honored our family and given you a great opportunity."

I kept my eyes cast down as was proper. The only opportunity a girl had was in marriage. Had my uncle chosen a husband for me? I dug my nails into my palms to steady myself. Four years ago, when I was only twelve and Maman first spoke to me of marriage, I told her I could marry only Pierre.

No, ma petite, *Pierre is Catholic. It cannot be.*

Then I shall marry no man.

"Fall to your knees, Marguerite, and praise the Lord for your good fortune."

I obeyed. I would do whatever Father told me, except marry the man of his choice.

"All of you on your knees," roared Father.

This was puzzling. Why would my fate mean anything to my brothers?

"Sieur de Roberval has chosen this girl to go with him to the New World, to Canada. She will be with the first to establish a colony for France!"

My ears heard, yet my head lagged in understanding.

Father embarked on a long prayer of thanksgiving. I looked up to see if my brothers had understood his words better than I had. All three of them stared at me with black hatred.

Dear Lord, I was going to Canada!

I'd be escaping from my father's house!

"Praise God. Amen," said Father, and we rose.

"Why her?" said Christophe. "Why not one of us?"

"Because Sieur de Roberval asked for her. Another young gentlewoman was needed to fulfill his plans for the colony."

"But..." Marcel dared to interrupt.

Father silenced him with a look. "Marguerite will go for us all. Captain Cartier has brought proof of fabulous wealth in Saguenay, the Canadian west. Marguerite's share in these riches will belong to the family. Through her the La Rocques will build a new Montron."

Ah. Now the miracle made sense. I would go, and they would gain. I didn't care if not one *sou* fell into my pocket. Let them have all the gold if I could have freedom in Canada. But how could I leave Pierre? My heart raced, and my head throbbed. Later, I would think.

"The ships will leave from La Rochelle in mid-April. You have a little more than a month to outfit yourself for the journey and a new life. You may bring just a small sea chest. No fripperies are allowed. Do you understand, Marguerite?"

"Yes, my lord."

"The steward will help you choose housekeeping essentials from Montron. And he will take you to Amiens to purchase bedding, linens, stuff for clothing, and a pair of boots."

4

"My father is most kind," I murmured.

"No doubt your uncle will arrange a suitable marriage for you in Canada. These goods are to be your dowry. If the cost of these preparations exceeds that which has been set aside for your marriage portion, then you shall reimburse the family accordingly."

I nodded. I was being sent to Canada to marry, but I would not marry anyone except Pierre.

"Damienne will accompany you," said Father.

"To Amiens?"

"Of course," he said. "And to Canada."

"To Canada?" I was dumbfounded.

"Where else? A young lady cannot travel alone. It's a pity she's only seventeen. An older, more stable woman should go with you, but Damienne will have to do. You may begin your preparations."

"Thank you, Father," I said.

"God will watch over you, Marguerite. My wish is that you will fulfill His plan by perfect humility and obedience to your uncle."

I backed out of the room to where Damienne and Isabeau waited outside the study's door. I could not meet Damienne's eyes, for all the excitement within me would explode. I grabbed her hand. She caught up Isabeau, and we ran to the top of the house and the safety of the small chamber we shared.

Only when we had bolted the door against my brothers did we dare speak.

5

"It is true, isn't it?" she said.

"I go, and you go with me, the first Frenchwomen in the New World!"

Damienne and I embraced. Silently we danced the round that Maman had taught us and Father had forbidden. We swept around the small room, pulling Isabeau with us. My face was wet with tears of happiness. Isabeau was crying, too.

Bon Dieu! I stopped abruptly and took Isabeau in my arms. The child could not live in this terrible house without Damienne and me to protect her. She was sobbing now in my arms.

"Perhaps you could come with me," I said.

Damienne shook her head no.

Damienne was right. I couldn't bring a child across the ocean.

"It is simple," said Damienne. "Isabeau must go to your aunt, Madame Clemence."

Yes, Aunt Clemence could be the answer. A little girl had to have some sort of mother. Could I convince Father of that? Isabeau was looking to me for an answer.

"Damienne has the better plan," I said. "You are too young to come with me to Canada. Damienne and I must find gold and tame the wilderness first. You will go to Aunt Clemence, who loves you dearly."

"Will Father allow it?"

The poor child already understood our father too well. Aunt Clemence had wanted to take us both in after Maman died. Father forbade it, keeping me at Montron as his house-keeper. Damienne was giving me a look and mouthing

6

"argent." Ah, yes, money was the key to Father's approval. Aunt Clemence was wealthy. She would take care of Isabeau, and it wouldn't cost Father anything. I kissed my little sister.

"Father will want what is best for you," I said, lying.

"And will you send for me when I am grown?"

"Indeed, I will send my very own ship to bring you to my golden *château* in Canada," I said.

"And we shall have fine furs and caves full of diamonds and rivers of gold in Canada," sang Damienne.

"We will be rich!" said Isabeau, laughing.

"Rich and happy!" sang Damienne.

"Happy, happy, happy!" trilled Isabeau.

I stopped. Happiness fled.

"I can't go," I said.

Damienne looked at me with saucer eyes. "You're mad!"

"I can't leave him," I said.

"Leave who?" asked Isabeau.

"My friend." I never spoke his name in her presence lest she innocently betray me.

"Don't be a fool," said Damienne.

"You know I cannot leave him."

"That is not what I meant," she said. "Of course you will not leave him."

"How shall I go and not leave him?"

"It is simple," said Damienne. "He will go with you."

It did sound simple. In a world of Damienne's making, it would be simple. Unfortunately that wasn't the world we lived in.

TWO

DAMIENNE HELPED ME PREPARE A SPEECH FOR Father, pointing out all the advantages of sending Isabeau to Aunt Clemence. I made sure to emphasize the money he would save. He wouldn't need to hire anyone to look after Isabeau, and no doubt Aunt Clemence would be delighted to clothe as well as feed her. When the child came of age, Aunt Clemence would find her a worthy suitor, relieving him of a burdensome duty. She might even provide a dowry for the girl. All the while that I spoke, he continued to write his accounts. I stood before him a long time awaiting his answer, or his wrath.

"You may send word to your aunt," he said at last. "Remind Madame Clemence of her Christian duty to the girl."

"Thank you, Father," I said, bowing deeply and backing out of the room.

Isabeau would be safe. I was spared that worry. Now, if only I could be sure that Pierre would join me in La Rochelle.

Damienne had immediately carried a letter to him about my leave-taking. But a frantic week passed before I could escape from the house to see Pierre. I raced to the north meadow, where he and I met as often as we dared.

I ran into his arms. He held me so close that our mad hearts raced together.

"I'm leaving tomorrow," he said. "I'll beg or buy my way onto your uncle's ship."

I kissed the tips of his fingers. "Thank you, my soul. How did you manage it?"

"My father favored the idea. Even if Sieur de Roberval is Protestant, other Catholics will be along. Besides, there's too much to be gained."

As the third son, Pierre could expect precious little in the way of an inheritance. In Canada, he might find gold and diamonds. At the very least, he'd bring back a fortune in furs. His family had parted with two hundred *livres*, some of his sisters' dowries, to provide for his passage.

"I didn't tell them that you were the real reason I wanted to sail to New France," he said, "though I wouldn't be surprised if *ma mère* guessed it."

"Swear to me that you'll be at La Rochelle."

"I swear it," he said, grinning.

"And on board my uncle's ship."

"I will be there."

I couldn't go without my rock. As Christ had built His church on the "rock" of Saint Pierre, I had built my faith on my Pierre since that day long ago, when he'd saved me from the vicious farmyard goose, nearly as big as I. My brothers teased him for helping a girl. Pierre didn't mind my brothers; he cared only for me.

"I'll be there," he said again and kissed me.

I wept, returning to Montron, but hid my tears and continued my preparations for the great journey.

Cook didn't want to surrender any of her kitchenware. The steward told me to draw up a list of what I needed and he would get it from her.

But what to ask for? What would we need in Canada?

Damienne went to her mother for advice.

"*Mère* said we'll need an iron cook pot, a ladle, a spider…" she recited on her return.

"What's a spider?"

"The iron legs to hold the pot above the fire."

"Oh."

"Two sharp knives, a long-handled fork, a small ax—"

"Surely the men will—"

"To split kitchen wood," said Damienne. "*Mère* said we'll need it."

Even in a land of gold and diamonds, we would be hard at work.

"She said to ask for the six silver spoons and four silver goblets that your mother brought to Montron."

"Father will say silver spoons and goblets are fripperies."

"They are your due, Marguerite."

"Anything else?"

"We must pack our sewing kit with care, making sure we have plenty of sharp needles, thread—fine and coarse—scissors, and all the scraps of cloth we can find."

We'd be so far from France, from shops, from farms. Could my uncle's ships carry everything we'd need to survive? Would he bring cattle, sheep, and hogs? Would there be peasants to build us houses and farms? In France, I'd need silver to set up housekeeping. Would I need silver in Canada?

Remarkably, the steward produced everything I asked for, *including* the silver spoons and goblets.

"Perhaps he didn't consult your father," said Damienne, who was as puzzled as I.

At week's end Damienne, Isabeau, and I went with the steward, on the road following the sluggish river Somme, to the cloth merchants of Amiens. The steward had strict instructions from Father about the cloth for us. It had to be heavy and durable, not too expensive, and of a *triste* color. Although the merchants had many beautiful stuffs in luscious hues, Damienne and I had to choose from brown, dark green, black, and something the merchant insisted was purple but looked brown to me. I picked the dark green for my gown, and Damienne took the muddy brown. We both had black for our cloaks.

"It's all the same to me," she said. "I am a seed to be

planted in Canada. All that matters is that my earth-colored dress keeps me warm and helps me grow."

I minded. To finally get a new gown and not have the hyacinth blue was maddening.

"The green suits you; it makes your eyes look like the emeralds of Canada," said Damienne.

"There are no emeralds in my eyes; they are as brown as your own."

"They have green flecks," insisted Damienne. "Besides, the dark wool won't show the dirt. And there will be plenty of dirt in Canada."

At least the linen we got was quite fine. I had a few small coins given to me long ago by Aunt Clemence. I used them to buy ribbon of garnet for Damienne, pink for Isabeau, and peacock blue for me. I also bought some bright-colored threads to embroider flowers on our shifts. The world wouldn't see them, but I would know that I had some prettiness upon me.

From the moment we returned to Montron, Damienne and I worked feverishly. We stitched new gowns and linens for ourselves. We also had to sew new linen shirts and collars for my father and brothers to store against the time when we'd be gone. Father wouldn't have to hire a seamstress for quite some time. Because we were so busy, Christophe and Albert continually came to us with some new demand, simply to bedevil us. We worked from first light, through the day, and far into the night by the smoky light of tallows. By careful planning and cutting, we were able to fashion two new gowns for Isabeau, as well. I didn't want her to appear a pauper at our aunt's gate. Late at night, when we could be sure my father and brothers were abed, I stitched pink roses on my shift while Damienne embroidered daisies for Isabeau.

Our work was nearly done. On the morrow we would leave Montron.

"Do I sew my trousseau or my shroud?" I asked Damienne that night, feeling the weight of all that might go wrong.

"What nonsense talk is this?" she scolded.

"What if Pierre does not sail with us?"

"Have faith!" cried Damienne. "Trust in the Holy Mother. Have you said the prayers that I taught you?"

I nodded.

"And did you say each prayer seven times, in the exact order that I told you?"

"Yes, yes, and I lit a candle just as you said. But I don't see how it will help if my uncle does not want another gentleman on the voyage."

"But he will *need* Pierre if you ask for the Virgin's help. She will make it happen."

"I still don't see it."

Damienne rolled her eyes heavenward and crossed herself.

"Mary, Mother of God, give this poor girl faith!"

She was right. I had faith in Pierre, and not much else. I couldn't trust, as she did, that the Holy Virgin and all the saints would watch out for us as long as we beseeched them in the correct manner. Neither could I accept my father's

Protestant faith, which seemed just another stick with which to beat us. Like Father, Maman had been a Huguenot. Hers was a simple, pure belief, one worth living and dying for. When Maman died, her faith was lost to me.

At dawn the next day we assembled in Father's study for prayers. Isabeau, Damienne, and I were already in our traveling clothes. Our chests were packed and waiting in the courtyard. Our rolled bedding was tied to the back of the carriage. There was just the formality of saying goodbye before we could be on our way, first to Rouen, to bring Isabeau to Aunt Clemence, then south to La Rochelle.

"Amen," said Father.

"Amen," we murmured.

Then Father handed me a small, worn black book. I knew it well. It was Maman's Gospel.

"Take this book," said Father. "Use it as did your mother. Let the word of the Lord guide you and keep you safe from temptation."

I was astonished. I never dreamed that he'd give me something as valuable as a book.

"Thank you, Father. I will treasure it."

"Use it, Marguerite!" he said. "And preserve your soul!"

I nodded.

He put his hands on my head and Isabeau's to give us his final blessing.

"Keep these children safe, Lord, that they may serve You and their betters in complete modesty, humility, and purity.

May they bring honor to our house and prove themselves Your worthy servants."

Then he turned back to his accounts, and we were free to leave.

My three brothers stood awkwardly in the courtyard as the steward and Damienne stored our chests in the carriage. At last Albert came forward.

"Godspeed, Marguerite," he said, looking far younger than his thirteen years.

"Thank you, Albert," I said and kissed his cheek. Then I handed Isabeau into the carriage with Damienne and climbed in after her.

The steward slapped the reins of the horses, and the carriage jerked forward. I set my face to the future. Montron had died with Maman. My home had been lost to me for well over a year. I felt a sob rising and suppressed it, for Isabeau's sake and my own. Later, there would be time enough for tears.

By nightfall we'd arrived at the grand house of Aunt Clemence. She fed and pampered us. And we slept well on great puffs of softest down.

"You must choose for yourself," Aunt Clemence began first thing the next morning. "Don't let your uncle pick your husband. Find out from the chaperons about the young *sieurs'* families. Don't fall for a pretty face!"

I had already fallen, but I kept that to myself.

"Take care of Isabeau," I said.

"I shall do well by her," said Aunt Clemence, "for your mother's sake, and because I love her as my own."

Isabeau was happy in Aunt Clemence's kind embrace, but as the time neared for my departure she cried.

"You will come back, or you will send for me."

"I will."

"Swear it!"

"As you, Damienne, Aunt Clemence, and God are my witnesses," I said and kissed her brow, "I will return, or I will send my golden ship to fetch you."

"Swear on your heart!"

"I swear," I said and signed the cross on my heart, scandalizing Aunt Clemence.

"Marguerite! That is papist!"

"It is what the child knows," I said.

Aunt Clemence looked disapprovingly at Damienne. "I can't understand how your mother could keep a Catholic in her own household," she said.

"You know Maman owed Damienne's mother a debt."

"Well, yes, the persecutions."

Damienne's mother had sheltered my own when the persecutions of Protestants began.

"Even so, Damienne should have renounced her church when she came to your mother," said Aunt Clemence.

The steward entered. "The coach is waiting," he said. Damienne stepped forward and kissed Isabeau, as much her sister as my own.

I held Isabeau one last time. Her soft arms wrapped

around my neck, her baby cheeks were drowning in tears.

"Come back!" she shouted as I left the room.

"Come back!" I heard as I climbed into the carriage after Damienne. *"Come back!"*

Poor child, how could I leave her? Yet I had to, for her sake and my own. If I stayed, we'd both be back at Montron. Only in going could I set us free. But Isabeau was mine; she was all I had left of Maman's goodness. I'd not leave her forever with Aunt Clemence. One way or another I'd reclaim my sister.

All the long way to La Rochelle I feared that Pierre might not be waiting at the quay. As the carriage bumped and jolted its way toward the sea, I fought against my worries and tried to bury the sad memory of Isabeau sobbing in Aunt Clemence's arms. Spring teased us by hiding behind low gray clouds and drizzling rain. As we came to the end of our road, she put on her finest raiment. A warm, gentle sun appeared. Everywhere were flowering trees, beautiful as maidens dancing in the wind. Jonquils bloomed, forsythia, and iris. All the countryside we passed was bursting with new life. Fresh beginnings.

"You must pray now," said Damienne. "The Holy Mother will listen."

Why now? I thought, but said nothing.

Finally the carriage climbed to the crest of a hill. Spread out before us was the busy city of La Rochelle, its harbor, and beyond it the limitless sea. Soon my fate would be decided. And I began to pray in earnest.

THREE

The sea mesmerized me as the carriage descended into La Rochelle. Its cold, salt breath rose to meet us. Beyond the busy port it loomed, a wet desert—no hills, no trees, no houses. Instead of going forward into its cold enormity, could Damienne, Pierre, and I run away? I'd heard of servants running away. Always they were brought back and maimed so that they'd never run again. From the safety of inland, I'd envisioned the sea as our escape route. Now that I saw it swallowing the horizon, I wondered about surrendering ourselves to it.

We threaded our way through carriages, carts, and lumbering farm wagons to the harbor filled with ships. As Amiens dwarfed Montron, La Rochelle made Amiens seem a pokey country village. Our carriage was not so fine as many, and my suit of clothes drab and out of fashion. How sheltered and provincial my life had been.

While the steward made inquiries for Lord Roberval's fleet, I scanned the quay for Pierre's bright grin and saw only the faces of strangers. We came to the very end of the quay where three big-bellied ships anchored. The steward reined in the horses near the largest of the ships, the *Sainte-Anne*. Maman's name was Anne; perhaps this bode well. From the middle of the ship rose a mast, as thick and tall as a great tree. Rigging and spars were attached to this and the lesser masts. Fore and aft, the ship was built up with castles, giving the impression of two peaks and a valley.

We stumbled up the flimsy gangplank and onto the packed ship. Crates, barrels, and boxes crowded the little bits of deck space not already filled with coils of rope, sailcloth, animal pens, and seamen. A cabin boy nimbly led us around the many obstacles to the back of the ship.

"Aft," he said importantly, "to the lieutenant general's quarters."

I followed Damienne's gaze to the seamen roosting like birds in the rigging. Was Pierre with them? No. Neither was he among the massive men-at-arms busy with the loading of crates aboard the ship. I'd been so full of my need to leave Montron that I hadn't given the voyage more than a moment's thought. I'd never seen a ship before. Now I faced its dangers. Ships sank. Men drowned. I reached for Damienne's hand, feeling as small as Isabeau.

We climbed two flights of stairs, steep and narrow as ladders, to the top cabin of the aft castle. It reminded me of Father's study. My uncle sat at a large dark table, littered with papers and draped with a brilliant Turkish carpet. There were several heavy, high-backed chairs, and a number of chests stacked and secured to the walls. Three men attended my uncle, and four more simply sat, looking bored.

Grim and stiff as Father, Sieur de Roberval was dressed in black, but his coat was black satin and his linen flowering with lace. He studied Damienne and me with hard brown eyes as the steward introduced us. Did my drab clothes meet with his approval? I wished there was some lace at my own throat.

"They seem fit enough," he said, judging us like oxen. He gave orders to have our chests taken aboard the *Sainte-Anne* to our assigned berth. Then he returned to his papers, as cold and busy as Father. Not one word of welcome, nor one extra glance did he waste on us once he'd found us suited to his purpose. The only difference between the brothers was that my uncle had neglected to sermonize. Perhaps that would come later. The idlers seemed to take a mild interest and nodded as Damienne and I went out.

"*Bon voyage*, Mademoiselle," said the steward once our chests were on board the ship. "May God bring you safely to your journey's end."

"*Merci.*" I nodded, wanting to beg him to take us back to the safety of land.

The cabin boy stepped forward to lead us to our berth. We were committed to this voyage, and still I didn't know if Pierre would sail with us.

We followed the boy across the deck and up a shorter ladder to a tiny dark room at the front of the ship.

Perched on chests, boxes, and barrels that crowded the floor were six girls and three much older women, obviously the chaperons. Above their heads swung a number of netted bundles. The tight cabin smelled sweetly of scent, a frippery my father wouldn't have allowed. A pretty girl slipped off her crate and came forward to greet us. Her gown looked very fine, not nearly as serviceable as my own.

"You must be Marguerite de La Rocque," she said. "We've been expecting you." She pointed to where our chests were stacked against the wall nearest the door.

"I am Berthe de Fontaine," she said, "from Burgundy. There is Claudine, with the gold hair. Our guardians are Madeleine, Giselle, and Antoinette. And those are the Maries—Anne-Marie, Marie-Christine, Jeanne-Marie, and Marie. If you call for Marie, you will always find someone." She laughed at her own joke. I could see more or less the shapes of the girls, yet the room was too dark to see anyone clearly except Berthe and Claudine. I nodded and smiled around the room.

"How are we to sleep here?" asked Damienne. "There's no room to lie down."

"These are our beds," said Berthe, pointing to the bundles above us. "We open up the nets and hang in them like hams in a peasant's cottage. It is very funny." Berthe lowered her voice to a whisper. "Wait till you see Madeleine in her net. She is like a whole pig."

"I heard that!" said Madeleine, who was indeed quite large.

"Is there no privacy?" I asked.

"Oh, no," said Berthe, "not on a ship. Be grateful we are not down in the orlop with the sailors, servants, and rats."

It would take some getting used to, sharing this dark closet with all the Maries for at least six weeks if the crossing went well, longer if the winds blew against us. At Montron I'd had a stout door to shut against my brothers. But discomfort didn't matter if only I could know that Pierre was safe on board. Maybe Berthe knew if he was here, although it didn't seem safe to ask her directly.

"Where are the men's berths?" I asked, trying to sound casual.

"The *sieurs* sleep in the officer's cabin, the room beneath your uncle's," said Berthe. "The servants and young nobodies are between decks, with the guns."

That's where Pierre would be. He wouldn't give his family name lest my uncle recognize him as a neighbor of Montron and grow suspicious.

"How old are you?" The blond one asked me.

"Claudine! How impertinent!"

"I don't mind telling," I said. "I'm sixteen."

"So old," said Claudine, "and not yet married?"

"No."

"You are the oldest here," said Berthe. "Except for the ancient ones."

"I heard that, too!" cried Madeleine.

"I am fourteen, yet I shall marry a fine *sieur* before the year is out," said Berthe. "Sieur de Longueval is quite handsome, and his family's estate in Bordeaux is quite large."

"A French *château* means nothing," said Claudine. "I shall marry the man who finds the most diamonds in Saguenay, even if it is the short and ugly Sieur de Lepinay."

"As Marguerite is the oldest," said Berthe, "perhaps she should marry first."

I couldn't answer them honestly, so I kept still.

"And is there a priest to do the marrying?" asked Damienne.

The giggling ceased. Damienne knew that my uncle would never allow a priest aboard his ship. She must have been rattled to say such a thing. Damienne stood as straight as ever. Only her eyes betrayed her. She was afraid, and it shamed me. My friend was following me to a savage land without the comfort of her church, and I had thought nothing of it. I took her hand and silently begged her forgiveness.

Most of the company would be Huguenots. Perhaps some of the sailors and servants were Catholic. Pierre certainly was. Would that comfort her?

New worries possessed me. Pierre would keep quiet about his faith, but would he lie outright if questioned closely? I would have lied about anything to anybody to be with Pierre, but I was without scruples and God.

"So, who is to do the marrying?" I asked to fill the silence.

"As lieutenant general, Sieur de Roberval may," said Berthe.

"And there's that old scarecrow, Pastor Renais, with much

to say on how the damned will suffer," said one of the Maries.

Berthe laughed and the other girls joined in. Madeleine tried to shush them, to no avail.

If we had to be cooped up with so many girls, I was glad that they were the silly, merry sort. It would make the voyage go more quickly.

"May we walk about the ship?" I asked.

"Only when the men are not working," said Berthe.

"At dawn and dusk," explained Claudine. "And occasionally the Sieur de Roberval will invite us to dine with the officers and *sieurs* in his cabin."

"As we sail tomorrow," said another Marie, "tonight there will be a great feast."

"What will you wear?" asked Claudine.

Did she think I had so many dresses to choose from? My new summer dress would be pristine. Should I find Pierre, I'd want him to see me looking nice.

"Let us wash away the dirt and put on fresh clothes," I said to Damienne.

"Giselle will fetch you some water," said Berthe.

The feast in the lieutenant general's cabin was as gay as a funeral. Every so often one of the young *sieurs* would attempt a story or a bit of idle conversation. My uncle would have none of it.

"And what is the point of that remark?" he'd say, skewering the poor fellow who'd dared speak.

Only the pastor held forth unchallenged. He was a thin, greedy man, devoted to his meat. We ate in silence except when Pastor Renais had cleaned his plate. Then he exhorted and sermonized until the arrival of a new course. Never having been out in company, I was glad I didn't have to match wits with the fancy *sieurs*.

The Maries suppressed giggles throughout the meal, even while the pastor delivered a solemn prayer.

The only time my uncle responded with a shred of politeness was when the Sieur de Longueval asked him about the ships' course.

"We'll head north to catch the trade winds westward. Although the captain cautions me that the winds may not blow to suit our purposes."

The girls quieted somewhat, attending to what he said.

"Once we stand out to sea, there's no landfall until we reach Terre-Neuve. We hope for a fast crossing. Then there'll be less sickness and"—he cleared his throat—"death."

The giddy girls fell silent. The bold young lords were subdued. Only when Sieur de Roberval rose from the table, retiring to his private cabin, did the mood lift.

The girls and their chaperons might walk on the deck with the young *sieurs*. Berthe wanted me to walk with her and Claudine, but I feigned a headache and sought out Damienne.

"Now is my chance to find Pierre. Will you help me?"

"Of course."

We loitered by the hatch nearest the forecastle and scuttled down it when no one was about. Between decks was close and dark, smelling of brine and unwashed men. The low ceiling forced us both to stoop. We clung to each other, afraid to move. Men talked and someone played a tin whistle. The darkness began to separate itself into shapes. We seemed to be in a cavern of crates. The men were more toward the center of the ship. How could we get close enough to see and not be seen?

I crept forward, holding on tightly to Damienne, and straining to hear Pierre's voice among the others. We moved one step, stopped, crept another step, and stopped until we were almost clear of the crates.

A hand reached out of the darkness and clamped over my mouth. I nearly swooned, but not from fright. I pulled him into my arms. My love, my Pierre. All was well.

FOUR

We left la rochelle on april 16, 1542, under sunny skies, with a brisk wind. The *Sainte-Anne* lurched and rolled with the waves, as did my stomach. Damienne and I weren't as badly off as some. Knowing that Pierre was near made the journey seem possible. I hardly minded the puking bucket.

I did mind the tedium of being shut up in our hot, stinking box with nothing to do. The women were expected to stay out of the way and do nothing more. Doing nothing quickly lost its charm. Damienne and I had wool with us to knit into winter stockings, but no one can knit all day every day.

The girls made up nonsense about the *châteaux* they'd have in Canada, the silken gowns they'd wear, and the balls they'd give. Berthe, alone, seemed to know some truth about Canada. Her aunt, lady-in-waiting to the queen, had heard

Captain Cartier's account of his explorations and had seen the Huron chief Donnaconna, brought from Canada.

I listened well to Berthe's stories, though they made me wonder. She spoke of immense forests filled with game, seas teeming with fish, and winters of terrible cold and snow. Donnaconna had told the court of a warm land, called Saguenay, the land of gold and jewels.

"How can Saguenay fit into the cold forests of Canada?" I asked.

"It is beyond the forests, at the end of a great river," said Berthe.

"The Saint-Laurent?"

"So it is hoped. And listen, there are spices, too!"

"Could it be one of the countries in the East, such as China?"

Berthe's eyes sparkled. "Wouldn't that be grand, to be the first to find the Northwest Passage to the Orient?"

If we did, indeed, reach the Far East, where many European ships traded, Pierre and I might find it quite possible to escape my uncle.

I still couldn't know how, but it gave me something to hope for. Except that hope didn't fill a day much better than knitting, and there were many long miserable days.

After that first night, I saw Pierre only once more before we reached Belle Isle off the Bretagne Coast. I had ventured out of our stifling hen coop one midmorning, desperate to get away from the chatter and breathe clean air. Pierre was several paces away from me, far enough for me to see the whole of him. He was pulling on a rope, hoisting one of the great sails. His arms were bare, already sun-browned. The wind caught his wild curls. My Pierre had become a man. The muscles in his back and shoulders strained against his shirt. His arms were darkened by fine black hairs as well as by the sun. Last year I'd teased him about the mustache he claimed to have. Now, I realized, he did.

I'd certainly changed in the past two years. "Filling out nicely," Maman had said from her sickbed. Although, compared with Damienne, I was more stick than woman. As I'd been growing and changing, so had Pierre. Why did it take me by surprise? Because he was so much a part of me, I rarely got enough distance to see him properly.

"Mademoiselle, the men have work to do," the gruff old mate said, shooing me back into the stinking cabin.

I brought the sweet new vision of my love with me and sat contented in the stifling box.

"Good heavens!" exclaimed Claudine. "Marguerite is smiling."

"There is nothing to smile about," said one of the Maries as she pulled back from the bucket.

Oh, but there was.

We were forced by contrary winds to the harbor of Belle Isle, where we rode at anchor for a fortnight. Lord Roberval spent his days shut up in his cabin with the pilot, Jean Alfonce. It was said that they plotted the navigation of the sea roads from Terre-Neuve into Canada and beyond. The less my uncle was on deck the better it was for us all.

We recovered from our seasickness, and because the men's duties were light, we were released from our miserable box. Lest we be idle, enough freshwater was brought from shore for us to wash our linens.

As this might have been our only chance to clean ourselves properly before we got to Canada, we washed and aired everything. To gain more time on deck, we volunteered to wash the gentlemen's linen. I think Claudine washed each of her shifts twice for the simple pleasure of being out in the hot sun and cool breezes.

The young lords strode up and down the deck. And with each pass of the laundry tub they lingered longer to flirt with Claudine, Berthe, and the Maries.

"You'd best keep those legs moving," scolded Giselle, the chaperon who took her job the most seriously. "The pastor's got his eye on you."

"The old scarecrow doesn't scare me," said Sieur La Brosse.

"Ah, but you should be afraid," said Berthe, teasing. "Only fear will save you from the inferno of the damned."

"What nonsense," said Madeleine, laboring toward us with a pot of boiling water.

"Not nonsense," said Claudine. "All of Pastor Renais's sermons make me afraid, therefore I know that I am one of the saved. If I weren't afraid, I'd be one of the damned."

Sieur La Brosse laughed, as did the other lords.

As silly as it sounded, I understood Claudine. She had simply stated what the pastor preached. I didn't believe in it—that the *Bon Dieu,* the Good Lord, sorted all humanity into the saved and the damned. Why would He condemn a newborn to a life of misery followed by an eternity of damnation? Being only a girl, it wasn't for me to know the ways of the Lord. But I wouldn't credit the pastor, my uncle, or Father with understanding God's plans for us. I couldn't accept their saved and their damned.

Once Marie-Christine had rinsed out her shifts, it was my turn at the washtub. Damienne brought boiling water, and I took a cake of soap from my pocket to do our washing. Our outer clothes were sad, dark colors, but underneath, most of the girls wore shifts nearly as soft as silk. Some were trimmed with ribbons or lace. I was glad that my plain linens bloomed with roses, to show off before the other girls, and Pierre, as well.

The old mate kept the seamen away from the women and their washing, but Pierre managed to station himself polishing the metalwork near our makeshift laundry when I knelt at the tub. Pretending not to notice, he merrily scrubbed the brass and took a very long time at it.

A nastier, yet necessary, business was washing our blood-soaked rags. We might find gold and jewels in Canada, but there wouldn't be a ready supply of rags for our monthlies. We scrubbed the rags in buckets of seawater, boiled them in freshwater, and hung them to dry as much out of sight as possible.

At length the winds were deemed suitable to push us across the ocean, and we left the shelter of Belle Isle. The wild, powerful winds seemed likely to send us to a watery grave.

The roll and lurch of the ship from La Rochelle to Belle Isle had been like the gentle rocking of a cradle compared with this. Our sturdy ship tossed as easily on the seas as if it were a wood chip in a maelstrom. Waves like mountains rose around us and crashed over us, drenching our little box. All of the fowl had been moved in with us to keep them from being washed overboard. The birds and women shrieked with each new attack of the sea.

At first I screamed with the women and hens but soon grew too sick to care what happened. During our respite at Belle Isle, I'd been lulled into thinking that I'd overcome sea-sickness. I was completely wrong. Father would have said that God was chastising me for being overproud. But why would God bother to turn the whole ocean upside down and sideways to punish one vain girl?

The weather turned against us, as well. Storm followed storm. The wind howled, lightning flashed, and rain poured through any cracks in the cabin that the sea might have missed. Thunder was the worst. It raged above us, shaking the ship with the strength of its awful noise.

I hardly thought about anything. I hardly slept, and then only to be tormented by dreams. In them, I continually sought something I'd lost. Isabeau often appeared, weeping and begging me to return. I never dreamed of those who could comfort me, Maman or Pierre. Occasionally I had enough energy to pray for immediate death. I vomited continually. When there was nothing left in me, I still retched, spitting up blood and bile.

Sometimes Damienne was well enough to bully me into eating something. But whatever went down my throat came right back up. I lay in my own vomit, too weak to do much more than shiver, too sick to count the days or know the nights. It all seemed one limitless misery and a terrible mistake. Why had I agreed to this hell? Pierre might have been as sick as I was. We might not have any life together in Canada. We might not survive the crossing.

Most of the other girls were sick, too. Although we were crammed together, I heard their weeping and moans through the thick veil of my own suffering and ignored them. Only Berthe, Damienne, and the chaperons spent any time on their feet. One day Damienne was trying to feed me some broth. I clenched my teeth against the spoon, no longer able to bear it. I was, perhaps, close to death. She leaned over me and whispered fiercely in my ear, "You have the backbone of a worm. How dare you give up life without a fight. Think of your future. Think of Pierre!"

She was right. I was a lowly worm. My love deserved better.

From then on I swallowed what she gave me, and swallowed it again and again.

After six weeks of this hell, on a clear day of relative calm, at the start of June, a seaman shouted, "Land ho!"

I was still too sick to walk. Damienne helped me stagger

out of the cabin and join the rest of the ship on deck. Away, to the west, was the shimmering blue outline of Terre-Nueve.

"On your knees," ordered Lord Roberval. "Praise the Living God for our deliverance from the sea."

His voice remained harsh and strong, but he stood unsteadily, his black suit hung loosely, and his linen was limp and stained. The sea had taken its toll on him, as it had on the whole company. The hearty seamen, the elegant lords, and, most of all, the girls looked ravaged by the storms and seas.

In kneeling, I fell. Damienne propped me against her.

"The merciful Lord has seen fit to save these sinners," began the pastor, and I lost interest. Pierre would be here somewhere, and I needed to see him. While Pastor Renais prayed, I twisted about as much as possible for a glimpse of Pierre.

"Stop," whispered Damienne. "You call too much attention to yourself. He will find you."

And he did. Somehow he crept through the others to my side. I felt his presence, and then his warm, strong hand took hold of mine under the cover of my cloak. I dared not look at him.

"Let us pray for the souls of Henri Moreau and Raymond d'Abbeville, taken from this life as they performed their duty."

They must have been sailors.

"And pray for the soul of Marie de Montmorency," droned the pastor. "May her youth and goodness lead her straightaway to heaven."

What! Had one of the sweet, silly Maries died? I looked to Damienne. She nodded, and a single tear drew a line down her cheek. Pierre squeezed my trembling hand. How awful to die before one's life adventure had begun. I'd come awfully close to the same despair that had stolen Marie's life. I lived because of Damienne and Pierre. The poor girl must not have had friends who cared enough to drag her back from death.

FIVE

We anchored in the calm slate blue bay of Saint-Jean, away from the tearing winds and wicked seas. Wide blue, innocent skies with fleecy white clouds mocked the storms we'd lived through.

Fishing boats dotted the bay. I counted twenty-seven. They had come from Portugal, Spain, and France to harvest Terre-Nueve's cod. They were the only white men in all of Canada. Their claim to it was just a narrow strip of beach for their shanties and drying racks. Trees, bushes, and vines reached down to where rocks and sand met water, or gave way to patches of marsh or golden meadows where wildflowers flourished. Sea birds wheeled above us. Blue mountains rose in the distance, above the carpet of forest. No church spires. No castle walls. It was as if we'd stepped back in time to the beginning of the world, just before God created man.

Yet men were here. Wisps of smoke rising into the heavens marked their presence.

"*Les sauvages*," breathed Madeleine.

"Cannibals," whispered Giselle.

I felt the hair stand on the back of my neck. Not exactly afraid, I was more excited to see the people who were such a part of nature that they disappeared inside it.

"It is so big." Damienne was whispering, too.

This new land hushed the most boisterous of the men, but soon a clamor reached us. The fishermen were fighting over who had the right to which fishing grounds. Bretons swarmed the *Sainte-Anne,* beseeching Sieur de Roberval to settle their quarrel by sinking the Basque and Portuguese vessels. My uncle may have been tempted to fire on the papists, but the king of France wouldn't have liked being embroiled in a war just because my uncle hated Catholics. My uncle agreed to remain in the Bay of Saint-Jean to arrange a peaceful settlement.

As soon as the *Sainte-Anne* dropped anchor, boats went ashore to find freshwater. The casks on board were almost empty. For days we'd been drinking foul green slop, more slime than water.

The men returned within the hour, bringing the sweetest drink I'd ever tasted. Never again would I take for granted the blessing of cold, fresh water. I eased my thirst, then drank for the sheer joy of swallowing.

"I drink your health, Marguerite," said Berthe.

"And I, yours," I said as she passed me the dipper. So it went; each girl solemnly drank the other's health. Soon we were giddy, as drunk on the sweet water as if it were brandy. Damienne hugged me, and we laughed and drank. We would have danced had it not been my uncle's ship. I caught Pierre's eye from his perch in the rigging and drank him a toast before Damienne could stop me.

"Don't be an idiot," she whispered. "You know that the pastor is always watching, and others besides him."

"Do you begrudge me an instant of happiness?"

"Never. I just want you to be careful," she said. "Your uncle frightens me more than the pastor's hellfire."

"I will be careful," I promised.

That night the Breton fishermen brought us codfish stew, flavored with greens and onions from the wild shore.

I greedily ate the delicious food, determined to get as fat and strong as possible. I wouldn't let death snatch at me so easily again.

The next day a miracle occurred. My uncle sent all the women ashore with a guard and the filthy linen. We were to wash it and ourselves. While the clothes dried in the sun, we'd be free to collect berries and whatever edible greens we could find. To leave the ship, to touch solid ground, was almost too good to be true. And there was more! Pierre had managed to get chosen as one of the guards.

Pastor Renais wouldn't let us go without a prayer. "May these first French Christian women to set foot upon the shores of the New World set a shining example for those who follow. Lord, watch over, protect, and guide them."

There was none of the usual snickering. Having crossed the deadly ocean, we understood too well the risk we'd taken. What lay ahead might be as perilous.

I stepped out of the boat onto the pebbled beach, walked a few steps like a drunkard, and fell on my bottom. The ground was hard and sure, but it rolled like the sea.

"Ha!" The mate laughed. "You've got your sea legs. Now you must relearn to walk on land."

The girls clung to each other and stumbled along the shore, wreathed in giggles.

"Hush," said Giselle. *"Les sauvages* will hear you."

"Les sauvages know well we are here," said Sieur de Longueval. "Shout or whisper, it is all the same."

"Les sauvages," said Damienne.

"Les sauvages," I said, marveling at the wild land that produced wild men.

We followed a little stream to a small clearing of bright sun and sweet grass. I was wearing my one clean dress, saved for this day.

The foul-smelling, sour clothes were tossed in the stream. We waded after them, pummeling them on the rocks and getting thoroughly, deliciously soaked in the process. Meanwhile, the men filled the iron kettle and set it over an open fire to boil the linens.

The work was hard. When all the clothes, including the

heavy woolens, were washed, rinsed, beaten, rinsed, wrung, and spread to dry, the women collapsed on the ground. I lay panting with the rest. Had I come such a long, hard way to become a washerwoman? What would Maman have said? At least her littlest was safe and spared a peasant's labor. Aunt Clemence would treat Isabeau like a princess.

The Sieurs de Noirefontaine and de Longueval had gone off into the woods with their harquebuses. Occasionally we heard the explosions of their shots. They returned with many shouts, and a brace of hares and three squirrels.

Madeleine, Giselle, and Damienne set to work skinning, gutting, spitting the meat, and setting it to roast over the fire.

"*Toowhit, toowhee,*" called a little gray bird. I looked up and saw Pierre edging his way toward the deeper woods, farther upstream. He caught my eye and ducked into the shadows. This was our one chance, and I must grab it with both hands.

"Damienne," I called. "While the meat cooks, come help me gather berries. Perhaps we'll find mushrooms, as well."

"Mademoiselle, do not go far," said the mate. "Remember, there are wild beasts and savages."

"Do not worry, we will go just to those berry bushes," I said, pointing to the edge of the clearing.

"Very well," he said and turned to chide Madeleine for putting the squirrels too near the flame.

"This isn't a good idea," said Damienne as soon as we reached the berries.

"Pierre went into the woods just there," I said, tilting my

head. "You pick berries where the others can see you, and I shall go behind the bushes and slip into the woods. It is a simple matter."

"It is not simple," said Damienne. "It is dangerous. Be patient."

"Please, Damienne," I begged. "We haven't been together this whole long voyage. Let us have ten minutes alone in the forest. *Please!*"

She nodded, defeated by her love for me.

"If anyone comes, call my name. I'll come out with my basket, and Pierre will wait until it's clear. I'm simply looking for nuts and mushrooms. *D'accord?*"

"*D'accord,* but—"

"Thank you, my friend," I said and ran into the shelter of the trees.

Before I'd gone far, Pierre stepped out from behind a tree.

He ran to me, and I to him, rushing toward an embrace. An arm's length away, we both stopped short.

The crossing had changed us. I suddenly felt shy.

"Hello," I said. "How are you?" Such stupid words.

He nodded. "And you?"

"Now I am well, thank you." I was as stiff as if I had spoken to my uncle.

Pierre stepped forward, took my hands, and looked hard at me.

"I thought I'd lost you," he said. "Don't ever frighten me so again."

"Never. Damienne told me you were hurt. What happened?"

"It wasn't serious," he said. "One of the lines tore loose and—"

"Let me see."

Pierre loosened the neck of his shirt and pulled it over his head. Across his chest was an ugly gash. I traced it with my finger, following its course to a point near his heart.

"I was lucky," he said, "unlike Henri and Raymond."

"How did they—?"

"One of the giant waves simply washed them away."

He shivered. I held him against me. Pierre was warm. He was my home, now that home was gone.

"I have missed you so," I breathed.

Soon we were kissing, our mouths starved for each other. Warmth became heat, then fire. Time disappeared.

"Marguerite!"

It was Damienne, and there was panic in her voice. My heart froze. We sprang apart. Pierre rolled away from me and ran, carrying his breeches and shirt deeper into the woods.

"Coming!" I called.

I tried to order my clothes and smooth my hair.

"Have you found any mushrooms?" She sounded terrified.

"No luck," I said, grabbed the basket, and went to meet her. She was followed closely by Giselle and the pastor. Lord!

"I told you not to go so far," said Damienne.

42

"You were right. I've found nothing and grown quite hot in the looking." I was trying to come up with an excuse for my flaming cheeks. "Good day, Pastor Renais." I curtsied.

He inclined his head while his piercing eyes sought out my sin.

"It is wicked of you to go off and worry us," said Giselle, emphasizing "wicked."

"I beg your pardon," I said, perhaps not as meekly as I ought to have.

"Come along," said the pastor. "The feast is near ready."

He and Giselle led the way back to the others. I held Damienne back a step and whispered in her ear, "Did they see anything?"

"I don't think so, but I did."

"Can you forgive us?"

"Yes. But I'm worried."

I took her arm. We were both trembling, though I feared nothing. My body quivered with happiness.

SIX

I WAS SUFFUSED WITH JOY.

As I worked, as I knelt at prayer, as I ate and talked and slept, happiness magnified my soul. Every breathing moment, I lived through my love. I was no longer Marguerite, alone. Pierre was in my skin, the only sight I saw, the only voice I heard. I tasted his kisses again and again. My arms held him. I was so full, and so greedy for more, wanting only to be again in his arms.

I don't think anyone other than Damienne guessed at what had happened to me. I lived in the world of the others. At the same time I lived in a world that contained just Pierre and me.

A few days after we'd come to the Bay of Saint-Jean, Captain Cartier arrived with his three ships. He'd wintered in Canada, awaiting Sieur de Roberval. Now he was as intent on returning to France as my uncle was on having him and his men accompany us back up the River Saint-Laurent. It led to an argument witnessed by all at the feast held for Captain Cartier in Lord Roberval's cabin.

"You came too late," said the captain.

"I was unfortunately delayed."

"For a year!" Captain Cartier's voice rose.

"That is none of your business." My uncle matched him in volume.

"My men and my supplies are exhausted. We must return to France."

"As I am the lieutenant general, you are under my command," raged Sieur de Roberval. "You will obey my orders."

At that the captain remained silent. Food was brought forth, the pastor blessed it, and the mood of the party lightened despite my uncle's fuming. Captain Cartier showed us gold and diamonds that he'd found in what would be our new home!

"The walls of my *château* shall be lined with gold," said Claudine, "and the windows made of diamonds."

"If that is the pretty *mademoiselle*'s desire," said Captain Cartier.

The girls twittered and cooed like roosting doves. The men badgered him with a thousand questions. The captain couldn't have been more polite, or kind, as he answered their questions. But I could see his heart wasn't in it.

"Have you found Saguenay?" asked Sieur de Noirefontaine.

"Not yet," he answered, looking grim.

"Will the *Saint-Laurent* take us there?"

He shook his head. "I've followed the great river as far west as I could. We must find another river to take us to Saguenay, but—"

"Let it be one day soon!" cried the Sieur de Sauveterre, holding his goblet high. And all drank a toast to finding the wealth of Saguenay.

The next morning, June 10, Captain Cartier's ships were gone.

"Coward!" cried the young *sieurs*. "Knave!"

"Infidel!" thundered the pastor.

My uncle said nothing; his black looks spoke volumes. I didn't think ill of Captain Cartier. He seemed simply a man worn down by what he'd lived through. Never mind the gold and jewels.

"I don't understand why Captain Cartier left us," said Damienne as we sat apart knitting. Her clicking needles paused as she furtively signed the cross.

I felt the worry she hadn't named. If Captain Cartier could not find Saguenay, how could we?

"But you are my greatest concern," said Damienne. "Your immortal soul is in danger. If only you could confess and repent."

I would not do that even if I could, because I couldn't agree that Pierre and I had sinned.

"We must devise a plan so that Pierre and I can marry," I said.

"Yes, marriage is the answer. But how?"

How, I knew not. "We've got to talk to Pierre. We need his help."

"No. I feel that we are being watched. It is impossible."

"Nothing is impossible," I said, "if you have faith."

I was so intent on my pursuit of love that I saw no dangers, no difficulties. It was the first time in my life that I felt anything approaching the faith and courage that came so easily to Damienne and Pierre.

At least I agreed with Damienne that it would be folly to try to meet with Pierre as long as we were at anchor. There was too much idleness now aboard the *Sainte-Anne*. People were at leisure to notice things. So we waited a few days until Sieur de Roberval weighed anchor and we sailed north around Newfoundland into the Gulf of Saint-Laurent. The land, especially on the north shore, looked even more wild and frightening than what we'd already seen.

Damienne got word to Pierre that we would meet in the evening, when the women were allowed out of their hen coop and there'd be a general stirring on deck. Then it would be easier to slip unnoticed into the hold—our rendezvous.

The stench was overpowering as we climbed through the open hatch, down below the orlop, down into the foul black hole. My eyes were stunned by the darkness. Damienne and I held up our skirts and clung to each other as water sloshed around our feet. The ship's creaks and groans were horrible down there, below the water line.

"Pierre," I whispered.

No answer.

"Pierre, are you here?"

A rat squeaked and ran across my foot. I stifled a scream and held tightly to Damienne.

"*Mon Dieu!*"

"Marguerite?"

Thank you, God. It was Pierre.

"Over here."

We followed his voice. And soon I was safe in my love's arms. We kissed.

"There is no time for that," said Damienne.

"We have to make a plan to be together," I said.

"Your uncle will never allow it. Why don't we simply run away," he said. "This country is so beautiful. The sea is full of fish, the woods full of game. What more do we need?"

Pierre's idea scared me.

"Berthe thinks Saguenay might be in the East, near China," I said. "Perhaps we can—" But before I could finish, our plans were taken away from us.

There was the thunder of boots above us, soldiers running toward the hatch to the hold.

"Holy Mother!" gasped Damienne.

"Hide," said Pierre.

We crouched between two large casks. I cowered in Pierre's arms. Giselle must have seen me with Pierre in the forest and had just been waiting for an opportunity to catch us together. The men stormed down the ladder and dropped

48

one by one into the hold. The timbers shuddered, and I with them. Lantern lights flickered around us. Rats skittered in all directions. We were caught in a trap. Lord, save us from my uncle's wrath!

The soldiers found us easily. Two held Pierre, and two tore me away from him.

"My love!"

"Courage!" he called as Damienne and I were dragged up the ladder. I had no courage, only quivering fear.

They brought us to the main deck, where the ship's crew and passengers stood in a ring around us. We were in shadow. My uncle and the pastor stood on the quarterdeck above us, in the last light of day. Damienne and I clung to each other. My uncle could do whatever he wished with us. His rage alone could kill me.

"You are cursed, Marguerite!" bellowed Sieur de Roberval. "My own kin, and one of the damned!"

He was casting me away from man's law and God's love.

"I'll not have you aboard my ship any longer. Your evil ways will infect the pure ones."

Would he send me to one of the other ships? No. That would be too lenient. What was he going to do?

"You and the papist procuress are no longer part of my company. You are no longer kin to me. Be damned!"

He turned away from me and began issuing orders to his lieutenant. Would he kill me now? Would he kill Pierre? Damienne and I stood on the deck, a chasm of dread separating us from the passengers and crew. They had backed away as far as possible lest they be condemned with us. None dared speak.

Damienne and I trembled so, it was a wonder we remained standing. If only I could see Pierre. As far as I knew he was below decks. I might find some shred of courage if I could just see his face.

A sailor appeared with my chest and bedding. He heaved it into the longboat lashed to the side of the ship. Another sailor came forward carrying a basket that seemed filled with food. He put it in the longboat.

Why would we need our own provisions? Would we live or die? Something was happening, something I didn't understand. The second sailor muttered "God help ye" as he passed.

Then the ship's boy ran forward with a harquebus and a bag of shot and put them in the longboat.

A terrible fear possessed me, and I still had no name for it. I looked around at those standing apart from us. The Maries hugged each other and wept. Claudine buried her face in Madeleine's arms. Berthe looked at me with tears flooding her face. The young *sieurs* were stone-faced or sorrowful. Giselle met my eye with a grimace of satisfaction, my betrayer.

The ship's ropes groaned, chains rattled. Was my Pierre in chains?

Dear God, why was the longboat being filled with provisions?

Damienne murmured, "Marie, Marie, Marie..."

Yes, pray. Call on the Virgin Mother. We needed her help. I couldn't think of any prayer. Was my mind too filled with terror, or was I indeed damned?

At last the lieutenant came forward and took my arm. His grasp was firm but not cruel. He led me to the longboat. The old mate brought Damienne. I was scooped up and handed to another sailor in the longboat. Damienne was placed next to me.

"Marie, Mother of God, Marie, Mother of God..." intoned Damienne, tears pouring down her face.

The mate and the lieutenant climbed in, and the longboat was lowered into the Gulf of Saint-Laurent. They were taking me away from Pierre.

I started howling.

"Hush, Mademoiselle," said the old mate. "It will do no good."

I didn't care.

"Pierre!" I shouted like a madwoman. If I was to die, I wanted one last sight of my love. *"Pierre!"*

SEVEN

WE APPROACHED A CLUSTER OF ISLANDS WE'D JUST passed, near the north shore of the gulf. There was little to see in the falling darkness—the silhouette of trees, a rocky outcropping, and the flat swath of shore. Anyway, my eyes were on the *Sainte-Anne.*

"Where are you taking us?" asked Damienne.

"The Isle of Demons," said the lieutenant without looking at us.

I remembered that some of the sailors had crossed themselves as we passed this island earlier.

"God have mercy," said the sailor, pulling on the oar.

"Christ have mercy," murmured Damienne.

The men brought the boat to the beach. They carried us, two limp beings, over the water, and took the chest and the small pile of provisions to a sheltering tree.

"Adieu," said the lieutenant, consigning us to God.

"How can you leave us here?"

No answer.

"It is murder!" I yelled.

Their mission completed, the men were already pulling quickly away, fearful of us, or the demons, or my uncle's wrath.

"Monsters!" I screamed.

I sat on the shore where they'd dropped me, keening as the longboat pulled away.

"Hush, Marguerite. There's none to hear you that can help."

"Pierre can hear me."

"He cannot help."

"What then of us, two women alone in the wilderness?"

What then, indeed! It was a question with an easy answer. We would die, and it would be horribly slow.

"Pierre! Pierre! Pierre!" I shouted myself hoarse and kept on shouting.

"You will make yourself sick," said Damienne.

"The better to die sooner."

"And leave me to live alone, for shame!"

"I'm sorry," I said and hugged her. "I won't desert you."

"Nor I you."

We embraced and wept. We had nothing but each other and despair. Night was coming on. Behind us was the dark and menacing forest. Before us, the gulf, the ships being swallowed up in night. We huddled on the bedding, with our cloaks drawn around us. Though the evening was mild, fear made us cold. I ceased my howling and wept quietly into my hands, unable to bear the sight of the world around me. Damienne fingered her rosary and said the beads between sobs and sighs. If my uncle had done this to me, what did he have in store for Pierre? A hundred horrid visions raced through my mind. I was up again, shouting at the ship.

From its black silhouette came an answering shout. In the starlight, I could see little; neither could I hear clearly. There were angry voices, perhaps my uncle shouting orders. Then there was a great yell.

Pierre!

And a splash!

Guns fired, and I cursed the shooters. Damienne came to my side.

"It's Pierre," I said. "He's coming. We must call to him, else he'll get lost in this darkness."

We waded into the icy water and called his name without ceasing.

"Pierre!" How many strokes from the ship to this island?

"Pierre!" Which way went the current?

"Pierre!" Was he strong enough to do this?

"Pierre!"

At last we saw him emerge from the darkness. He held a harquebus above his head and waded to us. Damienne and I went to him as far as we could. When he reached us, he was barely able to stand. We supported him between the two of us while walking back to the shore. He fell to the sand, gasping for air and shivering. Damienne and I wrapped him in the bedding and rubbed warmth into him.

"Make sure the gun is dry," he said when finally able to stop shaking.

Damienne took out some rags and wiped the harquebus all over.

"You have saved us," I said and kissed my hero.

"You saved me from the sea," he said and kissed me back.

"The gun is quite dry," said Damienne. "How did you manage it?"

"I just kept thinking how much we'd need it," he said.

"But how did you get off the ship carrying a gun?" I asked.

"There was much confusion on the ship when you two were sent away," said Pierre. "Your uncle ordered me put in irons, but the sailors are all my friends. None would touch me; neither would they let another near me. Jacques got the harquebus for me and this shot."

Pierre pulled a heavy bag out of his shirt. It was an oiled skin sealed with wax. "Chrétien and the cook got these for me." He pulled out two more bags that had been tied around his neck. "One is filled with seeds, the other with ship's biscuits and beans."

"It's a wonder you didn't drown, carrying all this weight," said Damienne.

"But how did you get away?" I asked.

"The sailors brought me up on deck with unlocked irons on my wrists and ankles. I think Sieur de Roberval was preparing to have me lashed, but first Pastor Renais must sermonize. The sailors stood close about me so none could see what we were doing. While the pastor talked, I slipped off the irons. Jacques handed me the harquebus, and they heaved me over the side of the ship.

"I heard you yell!"

Pierre nodded, grinning. "The water is very cold."

"The guns could not harm you," I cried. "You are here and safe."

"I am safe," he said.

He was safe. We were all together. I fell into his arms and began to sob.

"Hush now," he soothed. "Your uncle has done us a good turn."

"My uncle has sent us to the Isle of Demons."

"No, my flower," said Pierre. "This is our Eden. I shall be the new Adam, and you, Eve."

"And I?" asked Damienne. "Would you have me be the serpent?"

"Don't be ridiculous," said Pierre. "You are our friend. We shall catch a Basque fisherman so that you, too, may live in perfect happiness."

"Not a Basque," she said, laughing. "They are too Spanish. I will have a Breton to be my mate."

"And will that make you perfectly happy?" asked Pierre.

"Perhaps," she said.

In that moment I was perfectly happy. For the first time in our lives we were truly free. We could indeed make our own paradise. At the same time I was terrified.

We had each other and so little else besides. I looked at Damienne.

"Have faith," she said. "The worst has happened. Yet we are alive, and you have your love."

"Faith is good," said Pierre, "but it will not dry our clothes. For that, we need fire."

Fire!

I felt a new tremor. How would we get fire?

"Be calm, Marguerite," said Pierre. "Jacques and Chrétien thought of everything." Pierre opened one of the sealed bags and held up a tinderbox.

So we set to work in the darkness collecting dry sticks. The heavens above were very bright. Many more stars appeared in this part of the world, each shining brighter than it did in France. The huge bright night loomed over us. We were such helpless creatures on our dark island. I was afraid to let Pierre or Damienne out of my sight. Mosquitoes bedeviled us, but the wind picked up off the water and blew them away.

I'm not sure that I believed in demons. I'd never had cause to consider them before. Maybe the island's name was only that—a name. Even if there were no demons here, there was still plenty to unsettle me. I startled at every little sound.

Twigs snapped, a hunting owl hooted, its prey screamed. My heart raced with each new alarm.

I'd never been out in the night before. At eventide, I'd always been safely locked inside the stout walls of Montron. What I would have given now for a wall between me and the scurrying, restless night. I tried to hide my terror. It was shameful to be as timorous as a babe. Damienne and Pierre seemed fearless. Pierre was even whistling. If he could whistle, I could stop quaking.

When we'd gathered enough of a pile, Pierre lit the fire. I held my breath until the flame caught, then settled between the two people I trusted most this side of heaven.

"It is a fine night," said Pierre, leaning back, stargazing.

The stars did seem less threatening, softened by our firelight.

"Can we build a wall tomorrow?" I asked.

"Yes, tomorrow we'll begin," he said.

"Pity we've no tools," said Damienne as if it hardly mattered.

But it did matter. Aside from our little kitchen ax, there were no tools to cut wood, to dig holes, to hammer. Oh, dear Lord, how would we manage? I was so tired, almost too tired to be this fearful. I was hungry, too, though I'd supped on the ship. I didn't want to say so. It seemed we should save the food we had for true hunger. I was also thirsty. Now rose a fear greater than all the rest. What if there was no water on this island? What good was fire, or food, or walls without water? The gulf was saltwater.

"We must find a stream, come morning," said Pierre, reading my thoughts. "And that is where we'll build our house."

"Will we find a stream?" I asked, trying to keep the panic out of my voice.

"Oh, yes," said Pierre. "There is water here, otherwise there'd not be all of these trees."

He must have been right. It was only logical. I had to believe him. Pierre opened the jug of cider and raised it high.

"To Eden," he said, drank, and passed the jug to me.

I drank and the jug went to Damienne.

My thirst slaked, I let the glowing fire comfort me. I had Pierre on one side and Damienne on the other, yet I could not rest easy in our Eden.

EIGHT

～

DAWN SOUNDS WOKE ME FROM A TROUBLED SLEEP.
I sat up, heart pounding, expecting to see boats approaching,
men coming to arrest Pierre and start the nightmare all over
again. I saw no men-at-arms, only the enormous sky, wheel-
ing gulls, and low fog on the water. Would my uncle pursue
Pierre? I didn't think so. Like my father, he would reckon the
cost. It would cost him time and men to catch Pierre, neither
of which he could spare. We were safe for the time being.

Before me, far across the gulf, would be the dark coastline
of Terre-Neuve that I'd seen from the ship. Maybe a mile to
the north was the mainland. It had seemed to be all solid
woods and rocky shore. I turned to see what I could of the
island. Behind me rose a forest, pouring down to this shore
of sand and rock. There'd be firewood aplenty. A clearing
to the west led up to a rocky hill where a few pines fought

the wind. Perhaps there'd be berries in the clearing, nuts and mushrooms in the woods. If it was like Terre-Neuve, we'd find all sorts of game—rabbit, squirrel, quail, and grouse. We'd find fish and shellfish in the gulf and at the shore. We had the basket of provisions and my sea chest—a little food and clothes, although Pierre had just his shirt and breeches. I blessed Damienne's mother for her practical advice. The ax, my sewing kit, and cooking gear might well make survival possible. I counted up all that would sustain us, to gain a little courage.

Wind blew from the east, stirring the mist on the water. The ships had gone! My courage fled.

My uncle did not mean to set me in paradise. This was a punishment, mayhap the worst punishment he could think of. He meant this to be worse than death. After all, he hadn't planned for Pierre to be with me. How angry he must be that we were together, that our sin could continue. Our sin.

When we were children, Pierre and I danced in the May storm of apple blossoms. Was that sin? Father said so, and I had no supper that night. But Maman brought me warm milk, kissed my forehead, and said I was not to mind. Was I not to mind sinning, or not to mind my father?

I tried to pray for God's forgiveness and couldn't. How could I beg forgiveness for this sin—the gift of Pierre's love?

"*Bon Dieu,* thank you for my love's love."

That was my prayer. God gave everything. This is what he gave to me—exile and love.

"Bonjour," whispered Pierre.

I leaned down and kissed his salty mouth.

What had Adam and Eve done on their first day in paradise?

"First we must find a stream," said Pierre, "then a clearing near the stream."

"Breakfast," said Damienne, waking.

"Food," I agreed.

"Not the ship's food," said Pierre. "We must save it."

Damienne and I nodded. The ship's food must be saved against a starving time. We wouldn't put that into words. There would be many terrible things we'd not talk about. What would be the use?

"While you hunt for game, Damienne and I can look for berries over there," I said, pointing to the clearing past the woods.

Pierre nodded. "Today I'll shoot our breakfast. Later, I'll set snares and traps."

"To save the guns and shot for greater need" was left unsaid.

"When you go through the woods," he said, "mark your path with stones like this." He put three stones together, making a triangle. "Point to where you've been. Then you can't get lost."

"A good precaution," said Damienne.

"You can also look out for the smoke from our fire. I'll lay on some greenwood. It will burn slowly and make a lot of smoke."

"Others will also see the smoke," I said.

"There are no others," said Damienne.

"*Les sauvages,*" I said.

"If the natives come, it will be out of curiosity," said Pierre. "Maybe they will help us."

"Maybe they will eat us."

"We have guns," said Damienne.

She was afraid of them, too. Giselle's talk about the cannibals would have put fear into anyone.

"Should we bring one of the guns with us?" I asked.

"Can you shoot it?" he asked, knowing full well that I'd never even held a gun. Neither had Damienne.

"You will teach us," I said.

"Your first lesson after breakfast."

"*D'accord,*" said Damienne.

We each drank some cider before setting out. We drank sparingly, only to stay thirst, not quench it. Damienne and I headed for the clearing. Pierre went away from us into the deeper woods. He'd hunted with his brothers since he was a young boy. If there were game to be found, Pierre would get us a fine breakfast.

Our skirts were still damp from their soaking, and heavy and stiff with salt. But when I suggested shedding them to walk more freely in our shifts, Damienne was aghast.

"Not even one day are we on this isle, and you are ready to be a savage."

"Only to be more comfortable," I said.

"Hmph! What would your lady mother say?"

"What would she say?" I asked. "How would she counsel me in such a strange predicament?"

"Survive, Marguerite," said Damienne. "That is what your maman would want."

"Then that is what we must do."

As soon as we stepped into the shade of the woods, we were attacked by mosquitoes. Swarms of them buzzed around our faces, stinging us over and over. We screamed and smacked at them to no avail. Screaming was especially useless, as then they flew inside our mouths, as well as into our nostrils and eyes. We charged through the woods toward the clearing, stopping only once to mark our way. Our noisy progress startled many a rabbit, and the squat speckled birds roosting in the underbrush burst from their cover. Each time, Damienne and I jumped and cried with alarm. By the time we got to the clearing, we were both awash in tears.

We sat in the sun, free of the mosquitoes, and gave way to grief.

"It's no good crying," said Damienne. "We must stop."

"Yes," I said, as floods of tears coursed down my swollen face.

We vowed many times to stop crying and did not. In the end we were both hiccupping mirthless laughter and sobs.

"Berries," said Damienne when at last there was breath to speak.

Once we started looking properly, we found a number of

berry bushes, of all different sorts—some looked like black-berries, and some resembled raspberries. The fat red choke-cherries were the ripest. Damienne and I ate as we picked, filling our mouths and the sacks we carried. The crack of gunshot rent the distant woods.

Both of us jumped.

"Pierre," I said, recovering some composure.

"Our breakfast," said Damienne, grinning.

Neither of us could stand to face the woods and the mos-quitoes again. The smoke from our fire rose languidly off to our right. It seemed that we could follow the edge of the clearing down to a thinner stand of trees, and so to the shore. The shore would take us back to our fire.

We hadn't gone far when I heard a welcome sound—water. At the far edge of the clearing, by a rocky outcrop-ping, flowed a swift clear stream. I pulled off my boots and heavy clothes and waded into the wonderfully cold water in my shift. Damienne shed her skirt and bodice without a murmur and followed me into the stream. We gulped the sweet water. We bathed our poor mosquito-stung faces, and washed away the trails of our tears and the berry juice.

We were high enough on the island to see the shore. The rocky promontory formed a sheltering wall.

"Wouldn't this make a good place to build our shelter?" I asked.

Damienne studied our perch. "It is as Pierre said, a stream near a clearing. We'll bring Pierre here after we've eaten."

"Pierre hasn't had any berries," I said. "He'll be starving."

We quickly dressed and followed the course of the stream to the shore. We fought our way through a thicket to our fire. Pierre had spitted a rabbit on a long stick, which rested on two Y-shaped sticks, standing upright on either side of the fire. He was turning the rabbit as we drew near. It was already browning and smelled delicious.

I held out my sack of berries, now a rather sad mush but still sweet.

"You found our stream," said Pierre, his mouth dripping berry juice.

"And how could you tell?"

He lifted my still dripping hair off my shoulder.

"Poor you," I said. "The mosquitoes have been feasting." One of his eyes was almost swollen shut, and red bumps covered his face and arms.

"They are vicious. I see they've gotten you two, as well."

I looked at Damienne and realized that I was just as bedraggled as she, my face as puffy and red. I turned away to hide. Then it came to me.

"They are the demons!" I cried.

Damienne and Pierre looked at me blankly.

"The demons of the island are the mosquitoes," I said. "Look what they've done to us on our first day in paradise."

They thought I was joking. They laughed and teased me. I wished it were a joke. Yes, they were only insects, but so malevolent. Surely they possessed more than nature's share of foul purpose. This island seemed goodly, with enough and more to provide for us, to give us life. Yet alongside the simple gifts of nature lurked something else, something of the devil, something bound to destroy us. I didn't know it well enough then to put it into words. Evil hid here in the little things.

It chilled me even as I ate the rabbit and laughed with Damienne and Pierre. All that first day, and all the others following, I felt the ill will of our Eden. Every breath I took was scented with its evil.

NINE

~

The rabbit, quickly eaten, filled only a small pocket of my hunger. Then it was time to ready our few possessions for a move to the clearing by the stream. Before we left, Pierre banked the fire with green boughs, saying, "The tinderbox won't last forever." Meaning that we must protect our future need for fire while we could. "I'll come back later for some embers to start our new fire."

Our meager possessions grew increasingly heavy as we dragged and carried them upland over the rough ground.

"Oh, for a cart," I said.

"There is no road for a cart," said Damienne.

"Then a horse or mule to carry for us."

"There's no oats, nor hay for a horse," said Damienne.

"No smith to shoe one," said Pierre.

"No ale for the smith," said Damienne. "And the smith won't work without ale."

They laughed, but I thought it a sad game to joke about all that we lacked now and forevermore.

We got to the stream, flung ourselves on its banks, and drank. I'd never known such thirst, not even after the voyage.

We sat on the bank, resting and planning our house.

"Near the stream," said Damienne.

"With the rock of the headland protecting our backs," said Pierre.

"Away from the woods," I said, remembering the mosquitoes.

"Yet near enough to gather wood," said Damienne.

I nodded.

"A home needs walls and a roof," said Pierre. "How shall we build our walls?"

I thought of the thick stone walls of Montron and d'Arry, Pierre's home, built in our great-grandfathers' time, the labor of many men.

"Not stones," I said.

"Wood," said Damienne. "Isn't it obvious? There is so much wood here."

"Yes," said Pierre. "But how to cut and carry it?"

We didn't have a saw, only the small ax, suitable for splitting firewood. And there was no horse or cart to haul logs.

Pierre stood up and headed toward the rocky wall of the headland.

"Where are you going?" I asked.

"I'm looking for something, I'm not sure what...a possibility."

"Remember how we made pretend houses at Montron?" I asked.

"Yes!" said Damienne. "That is what we will do now!"

"Pretend a house," said Pierre, teasing.

"Find a house," I said.

"Something that could become a house," said Damienne.

"Yes, I remember," said Pierre. "We look for a cave, a hollow in the rock."

We walked slowly, studying the land between the stream and the rocky ledge. I felt a lightening of my spirit, a sense of possibility. We'd made many houses as children, mostly in the apple orchard where the crook of a tree served as our sleeping chamber, and the grass between two trees, our hall. When Pierre and I had outgrown the game, Damienne and I played it with Isabeau.

We found a cave, but a feeder to the stream ran through it, and it smelled powerfully of some creature we'd not want as a housemate. We climbed a slight rise, and there was our possibility. We all stopped at the same time, seeing it. Three slender beeches grew a few paces from each other, forming a triangle.

"Do you mind a three-cornered house?" asked Pierre.

"Not at all," I said.

"We can make stakes out of saplings, plant them in lines between the trees, and bind them together with vines," said Damienne. "Later we can fill the holes with mud."

"It sounds more like a fence than a wall," I said.

"Later, we can reinforce the walls," said Pierre.

"Then we can build a stone chimney," said Damienne.

"Let us at least get started," I said. I hoped to have some sort of wall to protect us from what night might bring.

Pierre cut away the low branches from the birch trees, so they stood tall and straight as thick poles. Then he cut down and hauled saplings to our site. Damienne and I stripped them of small branches and leaves. We dug holes as best we could, pounding sticks into the earth with stones.

"Why didn't I bring a shovel?"

"Because you meant to go to Saguenay, and not be marooned on a wild island," said Damienne.

Pierre helped us drive the saplings into the holes as deeply as we could. We bound the first sapling to the beech with vines, then the next to the next, to the next. We pushed and pulled obstinate vines in and around the trees and branches. I was no stranger to work. At Montron Damienne and I had labored as hard as the cook or scullery maid. This was different. My arms, my back, and my shoulders ached. The vines tangled in my hair, tore my hands, and lashed my face. Weaving walls was nothing like the simple pleasure of weaving linen into cloth. By the time we'd finished two walls, we were filthy with sweat, dirt, and blood. Pierre staggered across the stream with another load of saplings. He dumped them on the ground and collapsed beside them. Damienne and I fell next to him. We three lay still, simply breathing for many minutes.

"We need to eat something and rest," he said and kissed my poor raw hands. Damienne and I bathed our hands in the stream and bound them with strips of linen from our chest. We sat on rocks, dangling our feet in the cool water, and ate sparingly from our precious stores. Pierre would hunt tomorrow, and we would scavenge for more food. But we had to eat to keep on with this hard work. When we'd finished, Pierre nodded toward the rock above us.

"Let's climb up to see what we can see."

It didn't look very steep from the stream, but we were panting by the time we reached the top. Clearly the highest point of the island, it faced west, watching the water as it moved away from us into the unknown of Canada. The sun hung low in the sky, painting the gulf golden. Far away from us raced the tiny shimmering sails of Lord Roberval's ships. None of us said anything. I gulped back a threatening sob. I could, at least, pretend to be brave.

Pierre soon turned his back on the gulf and the ships, as did Damienne. I had to force myself to turn away.

"Look how fine is our Eden," said Pierre, drawing me close in his strong arms.

Our Eden was about the size of Montron and d'Arry combined. A pond mid-island and several small clearings were all that interrupted the dense woodland. On most of the shoreline, the trees marched right down to the gulf. I shuddered, thinking of all those mosquitoes. On the south shore our fire sent up its thin curl of smoke.

"That is probably the first fire ever seen on this island," I said.

"Let's call that shore First Fire," said Pierre.

"We can name it all, can't we?" said Damienne.

"Why not?" said Pierre. "It is ours, isn't it?"

How could it be ours? This island belonged to itself.

"What shall we call this headland?" asked Damienne.

"Mont Blanc!" said Pierre.

"It might be white," said Damienne, "but it is hardly a mountain."

"It's tall enough to be our mountain," said Pierre.

"I think our names should be true," said Damienne, "and not exaggerations."

"Here we can exaggerate as much as we please," said Pierre. "Here we are free."

Damienne turned to me. "Marguerite, tell your husband to be reasonable."

"My what?"

Damienne, who never blushed, grew quite red.

"As you and Pierre will live as husband and wife, I think you should be married."

"I agree," said Pierre.

"I don't disagree," I said, feeling my color rise, "but I don't see how."

"I've thought it over," said Damienne. "I shall marry you."

"Is that possible?" I asked.

Pierre shrugged. "I suppose."

"In an emergency, a layperson can baptize or perform the last rites," said Damienne. "If you don't get married, you will be living in sin. And since a priest is not likely to come here, I will have to do." Damienne looked stricken.

My poor friend. I would do whatever would set her mind at ease. It wouldn't be the wedding I'd once hoped for when Maman was still alive and well. For my wedding day, Maman said, she would make me a dress of silk, dripping with the finest lace, and plaited flowers for my hair. She would have ordered a feast for Montron and the neighboring villages. Here there would be no silk, no feast, no flowers, but perhaps my mother smiled on us from heaven. All that really mattered was that I marry Pierre.

"Very well, let us have our wedding here and now." I hoped God would forgive us.

"Our wedding vows shall ring out over the island, for all to hear," said Pierre.

"I don't think we should shout," I said. "After all, God can hear a whisper."

I didn't want anyone, or anything, to hear us. It would only tempt fate and hurry grief in finding us.

Pierre and I knelt, facing each other. Damienne began.

"We are here in God's sight to join this man and this woman in Holy Matrimony."

Pierre was grinning.

"As our Lord, Jesus Christ, blessed the wedding at Cana with His first miracle, may He bless this wedding of

Marguerite and Pierre. May He help them to be true to each other, to love, to protect, to grow in faith together."

Pierre took my hand and squeezed it. The wind blew his tangled hair into a wild halo around his head. Damienne's words, so simple and true, touched me more than the pastor's sermons ever did.

"Marguerite, will you take Pierre as your husband, to cherish him in sickness and health, through all of life's trials and blessings?"

We would certainly find our share and more of trials on this island. Perhaps we'd also find our share of blessings.

"Yes, I will," I said. Joyful tears filled my eyes. Through them, this strange new land sparkled.

"Pierre, will you?" Damienne's voice cracked.

"Yes, I will. Yes!" said Pierre.

"I cannot bless you," she said. "Only God . . . I can pray for you. And I will."

Damienne knelt beside us. "Holy Mother, watch over your children. Amen."

"Amen," I whispered.

"Amen!" shouted Pierre. He kissed me full on the mouth. He kissed Damienne. We hugged each other. Was this not the holiest, happiest marriage in the whole world?

TEN

———

WE WORKED SO HARD EACH DAY TO FIND ENOUGH food that we were always ravenous. I never thought I would be ruled by my stomach. Yet every day, every minute, my stomach demanded the complete attention of my head and heart. It ordered me to *find food, now!* Even when food had been found for the "now," my stomach wasn't content. *Find food for later.* To give the stomach its due, the food we found was never enough.

Pierre ranged all over the island, setting snares and traps. Often he didn't return until evening, and then with only small game, hares and squirrels. It takes many squirrels to satisfy a raging stomach. The fowl were also small, mostly bones and little flesh. Their tiny eggs weren't worth the search in the mosquito-infested underbrush.

We ate the little fish of the island's streams and hunted the shore for shellfish. Big fish rarely came close enough to the shore for us to catch them, and we hadn't a net to catch those that did. Once we speared a big cod with a knife tied to a stick, one fish out of the hundreds that got away.

All the creatures of our paradise seemed just as intent on survival as we were. I thought with longing of the easy food we'd had at Montron. The plump hens agreeably gave up their eggs each morning. And they made only a little fuss when Cook caught them to wring their necks. Pigs, loosed in the forest to grow fat on nuts, came willingly back to Montron for slaughter. I could live without pork and chicken, but I began to wonder if I could survive without bread. I began to dream of bread, great fragrant loaves hot from the oven, and the honey cakes Maman made, heavy with raisins and nuts.

While Pierre hunted, Damienne and I scoured the fields and woods for greens, roots, and mushrooms familiar enough to eat. We took particular care with the mushrooms, knowing how deadly the wrong choice could be. Several times the greens we'd gathered made us ill. One entire day the three of us spent either vomiting or squatting behind bushes, downwind of our fire. The seeming plenty of our paradise was a deception, the demons' work. How better to destroy us body and soul than to present a lush garden in which we starved?

"We have to get away from this place," I said.

"But where can we go?" asked Pierre.

"To Saint-Jean, on Newfoundland," I said.

"That is four days' sail from here," he said. "And we have no boat."

"Could we build a boat?"

"It might be possible, but if we could survive the voyage, what would become of us in Saint-Jean?"

"The Breton fishermen would probably hold us prisoner for desertion," said Damienne. "Then they would hand us over to Sieur de Roberval to be punished all over again."

Perhaps we had no choice but to stay here, although I was increasingly convinced that this was, indeed, the Isle of Demons. Only at night, in the sweetness of Pierre's arms, could I believe in a dream of paradise.

On what we called the doorpost of our house Pierre kept a calendar. He made a short mark for each weekday and a cross for Sundays. On Sundays we rested. Even our stomachs let up on their constant gurgling demands. It was our fourth Sunday on the island, early in July, when they came. Pierre was reading from the Gospel. Damienne often insisted that I read, too—although I preferred to rest, to listen and day-dream. Pierre finished his reading from Mark. Now Damienne led us in the Lord's Prayer. Although she couldn't read, she knew many passages and prayers by heart.

"Our Father in heaven, hallowed be thy name . . ."

My eyes cast down, I murmured the familiar words, giving my whole attention to "Give us this day our daily bread."

If only the *Bon Dieu* could give us bread this day and pro-tect us from the demons. It seemed that I alone believed in the dark forces surrounding us. Should I try to convince the others, or was it better for them to keep believing in paradise?

Lost in my thoughts, I didn't notice their arrival. The overlong silence and wild animal smell made me look up.

Seven savages had come through the woods and across the stream without the snapping of a twig or the splash of water to warn us. Damienne had turned white. Pierre looked alert but unafraid. Fear took hold of my heart and rattled it against my rib cage.

Gaunt and weather-browned they loomed over us. Small animal skins covered their loins. Feathers decorated the shock of black hair bound on top of their heads, and reddish paint marked their faces. They each carried a weapon—a spear, a stone knife tucked into the leather cord around their waists, or a bow with arrows in a quiver on their backs. Three of them also had pouches dangling from their waist cords. They wore nothing else. So different from us, I fought with fear to remember that they were men.

Pierre got to his feet with grace and calm. He extended his arms, palms up.

"Welcome," he said, smiling.

They watched him, their faces still.

Would they kill us? Damienne slipped her hand in mine, and our fingers knotted. Giselle had told stories of savage torture, slow killing that would cause the most pain.

"Pray," I whispered to Damienne. I was too afraid.

She nodded slightly, but I felt her trembling. Maybe she was also too frightened to pray.

Pierre bowed slightly. "Wait, please," he said and ducked into our flimsy house. I couldn't believe he'd leave us alone with these strange, frightening men, even for a minute. Perhaps he'd gone to get our gun. I doubled my grip on Damienne.

Two of the natives went in after Pierre. I could hear them rummaging around. Pierre soon emerged with not the harquebus, but our dinner. This he ceremoniously set before the wild men.

The natives followed him out; one carried my shift embroidered with pink roses.

"No!" I spoke in spite of my terror.

"Hospitality is expected," said Pierre.

"But they can't have my shift." My one pretty thing.

"They can have it, and they will. Please be calm, Marguerite, and this will go well."

I could not be calm, but I held my tongue.

After he set out the small fish we'd laboriously smoked yesterday, berries, and greens, Pierre went back inside. This time he returned with ship's biscuits and the precious jug of cider. This was food we'd hoarded against a starving time, though we were nearly starving now.

"Eat," said Pierre. And he held out the jug to the older man, the one with the most feathers in his hair who seemed to be the leader.

They squatted on the ground and ate up our dinner in silence. Pierre sat beside me, with a hand on my shoulder. He looked very much the proud host of the manor. Once every crumb of food was eaten, the natives sat back on the ground. They wiped their fingers on their hair and spoke low guttural words of what sounded like contentment.

Pierre rose quickly, went back in the house, and brought out three of my silver spoons! I was so angry, I nearly forgot my fear. Damienne pinched me and I managed to keep still.

Pierre bowed before the leader.

"Welcome to our fire," he said. "Let this meal and these gifts cement a friendship between us."

They seemed to understand. At least, the leader bowed in turn to Pierre and spoke many words in their language. When he'd finished talking, Pierre handed him my spoons. Then their stony faces lit up. The men smiled. They marveled over their presents. They drew close to Pierre and rubbed his arms and chest. They fondled his curls. Pierre laughed and returned their caresses.

Then their attention fell to Damienne and me. They held up my shift and laughed. There was more talk, and they seemed to be comparing our merits. Damienne met more with their approval. One of the men took her arm as if to carry her away.

Damienne let out a small cry, the sound of a trapped rabbit. Pierre stepped forward. Still smiling, he freed Damienne from the native's grasp. There was more bowing all around and rubbing of Pierre. Then they were gone as suddenly and silently as they'd come.

Damienne and I collapsed on each other in a flood of tears. The savages had come and hadn't killed us, hadn't eaten us, but they could. They could come back at any time. They could finish off what little food we had, and then they could eat us, too.

"Don't cry," said Pierre. "We are quite safe."

"You gave away my shift and my spoons!" I shouted.

"Marguerite, it is important to be generous with the natives. They, in turn, will be generous with us."

"But we have so little. If we give them our food and clothes..." *And the only pretty things we have, there will be nothing left to sustain us, not even hope.*

"Let us trust in Pierre's judgment and God's grace," said Damienne, petting me.

Very well for her to talk; she had faith. Dear Lord, Maman's silver spoons given to wild men! I pulled away from Damienne and went into our dark hut to weep in peace. I threw myself on the pine boughs that served as our bed and gave over to grieving. I heard Damienne say, "Let her have some time alone."

She was right. If I had seen Pierre just then, I might have struck him. Anger and fear had me totally enthralled. Everything I loved about my Pierre—his confidence, his generosity, and his good humor—infuriated me now. And I couldn't bear to hear him talk to me about living in paradise. This was not Eden. This was to the east where dwelled the monsters of the Bible, Gog and Magog.

I thought these black thoughts, wept and raged for a long miserable time. And finally came to my senses.

This was the greatest evil the demon island had yet presented, turning me against my Pierre. I could lose everything else, but I must not lose my love. I sat up, wiped away my tears, and went outside to beg the forgiveness of Damienne and Pierre.

Although it was the Lord's Day, we spent the next few hours trying to replace our Sunday dinner. Not knowing the whereabouts of the wild men, Damienne and I refused to let Pierre go off on his own to hunt. And because we were noisily trailing after him, the game had plenty of warning and would not be caught.

We gave it up in the end and left the woods to the ravenous mosquitoes. We contented ourselves with eating berries off the bushes and carrying back a few greens to stew.

"Teach us tomorrow how to use the guns," I said as we trudged homeward.

"Yes," said Pierre. "Tomorrow without fail."

"And *this* time I will pay proper attention," said Damienne.

Before, she'd shied away from the harquebus. No doubt the prospect of becoming a native squaw gave her enough reason to defend herself.

The wind shifted slightly, and I caught the scent of roasting meat.

"I'm dreaming," I said. "I smell meat cooking."

"So do I," said Damienne.

Pierre nodded.

We quickened our pace, arriving at our fire to find the waiting natives. A large stag had been skinned and was now roasting over the fire, tended by two of the younger men.

The leader stood and made a little speech, pointing from the deer to us. Their gift to us!

"*Aionnesta,*" he said, once more indicating the stag.

Pierre nodded and smiled. "*Aionnesta,*" he repeated. "Stag."

I was in shock. Damienne took my hand, and we managed a clumsy curtsy. The natives laughed.

Damienne and I fetched water and stewed the greens. The cooked stag was hacked to pieces and served up on plates Damienne and I had woven out of rough sea grass.

Our feast was ready. Before we sat down, Pierre bowed his head and spoke words of thanks to the Almighty.

"Amen," we said together.

I gnawed at my tough, flavorful chunk of meat. I licked the grease that ran down my arms and grunted in satisfaction like the naked men around me. I stole a look at Damienne and Pierre, hunched over their meat, as was I.

"*Cacacomy,*" said one of the younger men, and he put something on my plate.

I picked up the round, dense cake and nibbled at its edge.

"*Cacacomy,*" he repeated.

"*Cacacomy,*" I said, dumbfounded. Bread. He'd given me my daily bread.

ELEVEN

～

THE MORNING AFTER THE NATIVES' VISIT, I WOKE
early to a world shrouded in fog. I could imagine us somewhere else, Pierre warm beside me, our legs entwined. The
sea's salt smell might have been that of Normandy or the
gentler Bay of Biscay. Mist hushed the shrieking gulls and
crashing waves. I had never needed to see sea or mountain.
Montron had always been world enough for me. I sighed.

"I love you, Marguerite," whispered Pierre. *"Ma chérie."*

He kissed my ear, my wrist. Damienne snored loudly in
her corner. We made love. That coming together, the gentle
explosion of our bodies, sustained us more than food or
drink.

"Bonjour!" Damienne chirped, greeting us, and the new
day began.

Pierre went to check the traps he'd set the day before.

Damienne and I picked over the stag's carcass. We scraped

the hide, putting every shred of meat to boil with the head, the bones, and some new greens. The natives had also left us a few handfuls of cornmeal. Damienne would have thrown them in to thicken our soup, but I begged leave to make us some sort of bread. I mixed it with a little water and fried it on the spider with a piece of gristle from the stag's haunch.

Pierre returned with a fat woodchuck, our dinner. We feasted a second day on the natives' gifts.

"The bread is—" Damienne began.

"Inedible!" I said.

Pierre laughed.

"Next time I'll make porridge," said Damienne.

"Do you think *les sauvages* will come back?" I asked.

Pierre shrugged.

"Do you think they are still here?" Damienne whispered.

"They've gone," said Pierre. "I saw where their boats had been pulled up onto the shore and put out to sea again. There was no other sign of them on the island."

"Couldn't we ask the wild men to take us in their boats?"

"Take us where?" said Pierre. "Would you trade this wilderness for another?"

"Yes!"

"Marguerite, this little island is safe in many ways. There are no large wild beasts. The natives may visit, but this isn't part of their territory. I've looked; there's not any sign of their camping here. This island belongs to us."

"No," I said. "It belongs to the demons."

Damienne crossed herself.

"I think we can make the best of this," said Pierre. "Didn't we come here to start a new life?"

"We came for the riches of Saguenay," I said. "And to be together."

"We are together," he said. "We have an estate larger than Montron and d'Arry put together. Let us at least try this life. I will get more skillful at hunting. We will finish our grand house."

"Grand?"

"It is becoming solid," said Damienne.

We had worked every day, reinforcing the flimsy woven walls with stones. These weren't the massive stones of Montron, but big enough to blister our hands and strain every muscle in our bodies. Once we'd dragged stones from the streambed and set them in place, we filled the crevices with brush and mud. The roof still leaked terribly, but Pierre had promised that we would mend that in time.

"Today we will start making bricks," he said, "from the good clay of our stream."

"Bricks! But you were going to teach us to shoot."

"Do you want to shoot at nothing or finish your house?"

"I want solid walls all around," said Damienne.

I wanted to leave. But Pierre was right; leaving might not be a possibility. If we had to stay, I wanted a solid house around us first and then learn how to shoot.

After we'd eaten, he set us to work hauling mud from the

stream and mixing it with straw and sand. We formed it into lumpish loaves and set them to dry on rocks in the hot sun.

"How do you know about such things?" I asked, pausing to wipe my sweaty brow.

"Unlike you, my pampered princesses of Montron, I worked at d'Arry."

"Pampered!" said Damienne, hitting him square in the chest with a glob of clay.

"I never saw you doing heavy labor at d'Arry," I said.

"I would never let you see me so," he said. "And you spent little time there the past two years."

Once Maman fell ill two years ago, I hardly ever crossed the meadow to Pierre's home.

"While my older brothers lorded it over the servants and tried to gain posts at the king's court, I learned to keep the estate running, so that the peasants and my family had food and shelter."

"It should have been yours," said Damienne.

"Pity I was born third and not first," said Pierre without bitterness. I'd never seen him waste a moment on regret.

While the bricks dried in the sun, we tended to the deerskin. We'd preserved the skins of all the animals Pierre had trapped, no matter how small—scraping, stretching, and pegging them to the south side of our house. When they were dry, Damienne and I kneaded them soft and sewed them together as best we could. We hoped to make a cloak for each of us before winter. So far the skins had made up only one very short cloak.

"Do you think the deerskin will make Pierre a shirt and breeches?" asked Damienne.

"It would have once," I said. Such a short time ago he was a boy as slight as a willow branch. "Now he's such a—"

"I am a great strong bull! I am invincible!" he bellowed.

"Hush," I said. "They'll hear you."

Pierre laughed and caught me in a bear hug. "Don't fret, my princess. No one but you and Damienne can hear me being a fool."

"Fool bull," said Damienne. "Will you have a new shirt or breeches?"

"Breeches, Madame, *s'il vous plaît*."

We pegged the deerskin to stretch it more. Then we skinned, gutted, and roasted the woodchuck Pierre had brought back that morning. I was ready to collapse by the fire until the meat was done, but Pierre and Damienne had begun stacking our bricks in a circle. Every part of my body hurt and longed for rest, but if they worked, I worked with them.

We stacked the bricks in the shape of a beehive and set a small green wood fire inside to cook them hard.

"We'll make several of these," said Pierre, patting the hive. "One will be our smokehouse to cure our meat and fish. The others will cook our bricks. When we've enough bricks to finish the walls and build a chimney, we will use the ovens as storehouses for all the food that won't fit in *la maison*."

"*La maison!*" I said.

"*Le château* if you prefer," said Pierre.

"It is a poor little *cabane* at best," I said.

"Please, Marguerite, a little imagination."

"This time I agree with Pierre," said Damienne. "It is where we live. It is *La Maison!*"

I would have called it Desolation, but held my tongue.

That night Pierre kissed my raw hands and aching shoulders.

"Poor love," he said. "You were not made to know such labor."

"At least we were together all day," I said, thinking of the many days when Pierre hunted from dawn to dusk. By midday I would long for his body. I would need his voice, his curls, and his dark eyes.

The next morning Pierre began our first serious lesson in shooting the harquebus. He began by teaching us how to dismantle and clean the gun, how to prepare the powder and shot, and how to load it. This we did several times, until Pierre was satisfied we understood it. Then we emptied the gun. Since we could not waste even a pinch of ammunition, we would practice shooting without it.

Pierre pinned a small piece of white cloth to his chest.

"Marguerite, you go first. I'll show you how to aim, and you will shoot me through the heart."

"No!"

"Don't be silly! The gun is not loaded."

"I cannot shoot you!" I cried. "There must be another way."

"The only way I can see if you are aiming correctly is if I am the target," he said.

I shook my head.

"Then Damienne will go first. I don't think she will mind shooting me."

"Not at all," said Damienne, gingerly taking hold of the harquebus.

Pierre showed her how to hold it firmly against her shoulder.

"The gun will kick back when it goes off. You must be prepared, else it will knock you backward and you'll miss your shot."

Damienne nodded and planted her feet firmly on the ground.

"Sight along the top of the barrel," he said. "Aim an inch lower than that. Squeeze the trigger slowly. *Tu comprends?*"

"I understand."

"*Bien!*" Pierre stepped back fifteen paces. "Ready? Aim. Fire!"

Damienne took her time aiming and squeezed the trigger.

"Aim lower," said Pierre. "Try again."

Again.

"Too high this time. Again."

Many more times Damienne shot my beloved with an empty gun while I berated myself. It was only pretend. It did not hurt Pierre in any way. I wanted to learn to shoot. I had to learn. What if the wild men came back when Pierre was not around? What if they weren't so friendly? What if they were too friendly?

"Excellent, Damienne!" said Pierre at last. "You are ready to try it with shot." He started to put the target on a tree.

"It is my turn to practice," I said.

"Good!" said Pierre. "So, now you are ready to shoot me?"

"Yes," I said, forcing a smile.

He came close and put his arms around me to get the gun in the right position and show me how to aim. Then he stepped back, the white target back on his chest.

"Ready?"

"Yes."

"Aim. Fire!"

I pointed the gun at my love's heart, held my breath, and pulled the trigger.

"Bang!" He shouted and fell to the ground.

I knew it was a joke. I knew the gun wasn't loaded. But terror took hold of me.

He lay on the ground without moving.

"Pierre," I said.

No response, not even a twitch.

I ran to him, flung myself on the ground, and shook him. Pierre started to laugh. And I hit him. Hard.

"Ow! Marguerite, I was just teasing you," he said, holding the side of his face.

"It wasn't funny!"

A line of blood trickled out of the corner of his mouth.

"Mon Dieu!" I screamed. "What have I done?"

"Nothing," he said.

"Pierre, you should know better," said Damienne, hugging me. "We can't even joke about . . . Look, she's hysterical."

I was shaking and sobbing.

"Marguerite, don't cry," he said. "It is all right."

"No, it isn't. I hit you. That is unforgivable. It is this demon island. We've got to leave here."

They both looked at me as if I were mad.

"Can't you feel it?"

"No," said Damienne. "It is hard, but not evil. We just need to get used to it."

"We cannot get used to starving."

"We will not starve," said Pierre. "There is plenty all around us. If the natives can kill a deer, so can I."

"And we will grow some of our own food," said Damienne. "Remember, we have seeds."

Perhaps they couldn't feel the evil as I did. They were God's chosen, and He'd spared them even the awareness of evil. I was not so good.

"Can we at least try to make a boat?"

"If it will make you happy, we will build a boat," said Pierre.

And I knew he would do it, to make me happy, and not because he felt the danger. How could I convince him that the danger was real?

TWELVE

━━━◆━━━

I COULD NOT GET PIERRE AND DAMIENNE STARTED on building a boat.

"A boat is a good idea," said Pierre, humoring me. "Perhaps we can work on one over the winter and go exploring in the spring."

"Perhaps we will be the first to find Saguenay," said Damienne. "And all the gold and emeralds will be ours, and they"—she meant my uncle and his company—"they will find only the stones of Canada!" She spat on the ground.

Damienne rarely lost her temper, and here she was spitting! Pierre fell over, laughing at her.

So the boat, our possibility of escape from this place, became a sort of joke and was put off until all the other pressing work for our survival would be done.

That work would never be done. I wanted to jump up and

down, to scream and rage that we could not survive here. No matter how thick and strong we built the walls of our house, it could not protect us from the evil that reigned in our Eden.

And what if I should rage and shout? It would only give them cause for worry, not about the island, but about me. They already worried enough about me. They were stronger, more solid than I was in body and spirit. And whenever I tried to tell them about the danger around us, they would exchange looks. I could almost hear their thoughts: *This life is too hard on Marguerite. We must spare her as much as we can. We must reassure her.*

So they would humor and coddle me, take on extra work, and try to give me more food. They did everything for me except truly listen.

By mid-August we'd been on the island for seven weeks and finished our little house. At least all the walls were solid, and the roof did not leak. We'd made a stout door that hung from leather hinges. We could bar it from the inside with a heavy branch.

As long as the weather was warm, we'd keep our fire outside. Soon we'd need to bring it in. Building the fireplace and chimney was our current backbreaking labor. We'd left an arched opening in the stone wall on the north-facing side of our house. We began making a beehive of stone on the outside of this. When it was about chest high, we filled all crevices with mud, cut away the inside wall of saplings, and started a small greenwood fire inside the beehive hearth to bake the mud. While we waited for that to harden, we went on with our brick making, accumulating quite a pile beside our chimney-to-be.

Pierre had left footholds on the outside of the fireplace so that he could climb on top of it to build up the chimney. Damienne and I handed up to him stones, bricks, and mud to cement them together. Each night we lit the fire to bake the part of the chimney we'd built during the day.

It was almost impossible to sleep inside; there was so much smoke.

"Let's sleep out under the beautiful stars," said Pierre.

"Never," said Damienne. And I agreed.

So we slept in the smoke, and Pierre and Damienne made awful jokes about what would cook first, the chimney or us.

When we weren't building the chimney, or digging, planting, and weeding a small garden we hoped would bear spinach and rye before the first frost, Pierre taught us how to make and set snares and traps. The three of us hunting ought to have provided us with three times the amount of game.

It meant going into the depths of the woods where the mosquitoes were most vicious and the island's evil so concentrated that I could hardly breathe. Not even there did Pierre or Damienne notice anything other than the nuisance of insects. At least the smoke that clung to our hair and clothes drove the mosquitoes away. It also warned the game of our presence and drove them away, too.

Fear of the demons made me clumsy. I stepped in the snare we'd just so painstakingly set.

"It is not a problem," said Pierre. "We simply…" and he began again.

I learned slowly and never got very good at it. Yet, as the days of our lessons became weeks, we did have more to eat, and more food to store. I even became slightly less terrified of the woods. I let Damienne leave my side to set her own snares. There were days when I could almost convince myself that the evil I feared was all in my head.

The food we were accumulating began to attract scavengers. A fox nearly got the supply of dried fish we'd hung from the highest point of our roof. Damienne shot him cleanly through the eye and claimed his fur for herself. He looked scraggly lying dead on the ground, but by the time Damienne was through cleaning and brushing the pelt, he made a handsome fur collar for her cloak.

"Marguerite! Damienne!" On Tuesday in the first week of September Pierre came crashing into the clearing. I'd never seen him so excited.

"What's wrong?" I cried.

"Nothing." He was grinning and breathing hard. "A deer! Come!"

Damienne grabbed the knife and I the small ax and raced after him into the woods.

"My hero!" I said when I saw the trapped doe. I hugged Pierre and screamed with delight. I grabbed Damienne and twirled her around and around. "Rich!" I sang. "We are rich!"

In my earlier life I might have felt pity for the beautiful creature fighting to free herself. Not now.

Pierre laughed at me. "You see," he said, "I have gotten more skillful and a little bit lucky. This is our first deer but not our last."

This would be several meals for us, fresh roasted meat for now and dried smoked strips for later. Pierre would have his deerskin shirt and breeches, too. As wonderful as the natives' deer had been, this was better. This was our own. Pierre cut the deer's throat, and Damienne caught the blood in an oiled sack.

I stood still.

"Listen," I said.

"What?" asked Damienne.

"Nothing," I said. The woods spoke in bird song and squirrel chatter—perfectly natural sounds. My heart beat steadily, my breath came easily. There was peace around me, peace in my heart. I felt an inkling of safety. Was it possible? Had the demons been exorcised by Damienne's faith and Pierre's goodness? I put that thought away for later.

The three of us went to work. We tied the deer's front and hind legs together, cut down a sapling, and used it as a pole to carry the deer back to our stream. There, we gutted, skinned, and cut the meat into pieces small enough to cook. Nothing was wasted. We needed it all: entrails for sausages, blood for pudding, bladder to make a bag, hooves for tools, heart to stew, hide for clothing, and precious meat. We sang as we worked. Usually Damienne and Pierre sang and I listened. Now, I sang with them. For the first time, I had hope.

Pierre was true to his word. He brought down another deer the next week and the next. We built a bigger smoke-house. Damienne and I began fashioning deerskin shifts for ourselves, shorter and lighter than our woolen clothes and less cumbersome in the woods.

We were well, even gaining some flesh, and certainly mus-cle. Only once during the entire month of September was I reminded of the island's demons when one night something we ate made us all quite ill. Damienne and I pondered it the next day when our bowels had calmed down.

"Weren't those the same greens we'd eaten before with-out incident?" I asked.

She nodded.

"Perhaps something else slipped in with them," she said.

"But we're so careful about that," I said. I examined each herb I picked, then had Damienne sort through my basket before anything went into the pot.

"We must have missed something."

"It isn't a good plan to poison your best hunter," said Pierre. He'd been sicker than either of us, and he still looked pale.

"Soon we will have our own spinach and onions," said Damienne. "And we won't have to rely on the wild things."

That was the one cloud in all of our beautiful September.

October began bright and clear. Our chimney was finished and drew quite well. Sometimes we lit a fire for the joy of having a hearth of our own. Love grew, nourished each day with sun and laughter, and each night with the continually surprising pleasure Pierre and I found together. I felt guilty for having so much more than Damienne, but she never grudged us an instant of happiness. Only when I thought of Isabeau—and Damienne and Pierre thought of their families—were we sad. I began to pray in earnest, thanking God for caring for us, for turning my uncle's curse into a blessing. I never ceased to worry about the winter ahead, the possibility of the natives' return or the arrival of other savages, our continuing need for food, and so on. But I was forced by happiness to rest my worries.

Near sunset early in October, Damienne and I had the cook pot simmering with a stew of fish that we had caught in a net fashioned out of knitting wool and vines. While waiting for Pierre's return from his daylong hunt, we were attempting to comb out the matted mess of each other's hair.

"I cannot bear this anymore," said Damienne.

She disappeared into our house and emerged with the sewing scissors.

"You wouldn't!"

"I would. I will," she said, grabbed a hank of her hair, and lopped it off just above her shoulder.

"Now you cut off the rest."

"Are you sure?"

"Yes. Just do it quickly before I am not sure."

My hands trembled, but I obeyed. Damienne's hair fell, and her tears flowed. Soon I was crying with her.

"Now cut my hair," I said.

She looked at me, grieved.

"Yes, do it. We are sisters in this as in all things."

Once she'd cut away my tangled mane, I swung my head and felt the glorious lightness of it. "Why ever didn't we do this before?" I said. "It's wonderful."

Damienne sniffed. She touched her hair and mine and smiled.

"You are beautiful, Marguerite."

We heard Pierre's approach.

"What will he say!" I said.

We looked at each other and giggled.

"Mon Dieu!" he said, dropping a brace of rabbits at our feet. "This morning I left two women, and I return to find two boys!" He slowly circled us.

"Not bad. Not bad at all."

Damienne blushed scarlet. I felt the color rising in my face, too.

"Will you be wearing breeches next?" he asked.

"Perhaps," said Damienne. "If it suits us."

"Damienne!" I never thought I'd hear her say such a thing.

"We've already given up our long skirts, and come winter we'll need something to warm our legs."

"Your mothers would be shocked, not I," said Pierre. "We are in a new land, we must live in new ways."

"Amen," said Damienne.

Pierre laughed. "So, what soup do you cook tonight? It smells like my old boots."

Damienne hit him lightly with her ladle.

"For you, old boot. Marguerite and I will have sorrel, or whatever this bitter green is called."

"In truth, I'm not so hungry this evening," he said, rubbing his stomach.

"What is it?" I was alarmed. Pierre was never not hungry.

"Nothing. Perhaps I've merely eaten too much of Damienne's sorrel."

Before the rabbits had cooked, Pierre was vomiting a foul black stream.

I held his head while he vomited. Damienne fetched water and a cloth to clean his face and cool his brow.

"Pierre, what happened?"

"I ate some greens and mushrooms, the same kind that you cook," he said.

Damienne looked at me and shrugged.

"He'll rid himself of the poison, and it will pass. Pierre has suffered this before."

We half carried, half dragged him into the house, where he continued to vomit throughout the night. The vomiting brought no relief, and most of the time he was doubled over in pain.

"My poor darling." I felt so helpless. There was nothing we could do to soothe him that long awful night.

Come morning, he was no better. Damienne brewed an infusion of mint, which went untasted.

By midday, the vomiting stopped. By dusk the pain was gone. He drank Damienne's brew and smiled.

"Eh bien!" he said, still pale, but not as gray-green as he'd been. "I will be more careful about what I put in my mouth."

Damienne brought warm water and left me to bathe him. I trembled as I washed away the sour smell of his body.

"It's all right now, Marguerite," he said. "I will be fine."

THIRTEEN

~

THAT NIGHT PIERRE SEEMED COMPLETELY recovered. He drank Damienne's infusion, kissed me, and demanded food.

Damienne laughed and petted him. "You see," she said, "our Pierre is quite well. By tomorrow he'll be as strong as ever."

"No work tomorrow," said Pierre. "We deserve a holiday."

"Yes," said Damienne, "a day of rest and thankfulness."

She would spend the day in a patch of sunlight, murmuring over her rosary. I would be content to simply doze in my love's arms. Although, if Pierre had some expedition in mind, I'd gladly join him. I'd do anything that would please my love.

In the depth of night I felt his hand on mine. Usually a deep sleeper, I woke instantly and fully at his touch. We embraced. I was so grateful for his return to health. Passion quickly brought us to a point where he and I ceased to be separate beings.

"My darling." I sighed, and sank back into blissful sleep.

The next day Pierre surprised me by wanting to sit quietly by our fire most of the day. Only at dusk did we venture to the top of Mont Blanc to watch the sky grow rosy with the setting sun. The water glittered golden. A cool wind blew off the water, but the last rays of the sunlight held warmth and I was wrapped in Pierre's arms.

"I think we've found our Saguenay," he whispered in my ear.

That evening he refused food and fell asleep at nightfall.

"Don't worry," said Damienne. "He was very ill. It may take a few days for him to completely recover. Rest will heal him."

I lay restlessly beside him, trying to read his sleeping face for health or sickness by the faint glow of our fire.

"Sleep," he said, catching me at my vigil.

"You sleep," I said.

He closed his eyes, but I felt his wakefulness beside me. The morning light showed him pale and haggard.

"I shall fix you another infusion of mint," said Damienne.

Pierre nodded—no playful banter, no teasing.

"Today must be a holiday, too," he said. "I am loath to leave my soft bed."

I stayed with him, and we both dozed throughout the morning. I woke to find Damienne sitting beside us, her face lined with worry.

"What is it?" I whispered, sitting up.

She nodded toward Pierre, and I saw his face gone yellow.

"What does it mean?"

"I don't know. Perhaps some poison remains in his body."

After a time his eyes opened, but he didn't seem to see us.

"Pierre," I said and kissed his cheek.

"Marguerite," he said. "My love."

The next instant he went rigid. His eyes rolled back in his head, and his body began a terrible twitching.

"Convulsions," said Damienne. Her voice was calm in a way I'd never heard before.

"What can we do?"

She looked me square in the eye.

"Hold his hand" was all she said, but I knew the rest.

"Dear God," I prayed. "Help him! Save Pierre!"

Damienne rubbed his arms and legs, murmuring her own prayers. We rubbed him and prayed. I don't know how long it lasted.

Pierre shuddered, groaned, and lay still.

"Help him!" I shrieked.

Damienne leaned over him, her cheek to his mouth. She felt his chest. She tore open his shirt and put her ear to his heart.

"What is it?" I was trembling all over.

"His heart has stopped," she said.

I pulled her away from him and listened. Nothing. I could hear nothing, feel nothing but stillness. I grabbed his shoulders and began shaking him furiously.

"Pierre!" I shouted. *"Pierre. Stop this! Pierre!"*

Damienne dragged me away from him and slapped me hard.

"Marguerite. Oh, my friend."

She took me in her arms and held me tight until I could understand that Pierre was dead.

I hated everything.

I was mad with grief. Raving. Insane. Furious. I don't know how Damienne stood me. I howled without cease, tore my clothes, my hair.

I attacked Pierre, my beloved. I screamed, "Get up! Get up! Stop joking!" I beat on his chest.

Damienne prayed, letting me rage through the night. At dawn she said, "Stop now, Marguerite. We must prepare him."

Her calmness penetrated my madness. I nodded, exhausted.

We stripped away his clothes and washed his body. There was my beautiful Pierre, the sweet boy who'd been my friend since birth. My joy. My man.

"Pierre," said Damienne, speaking softly as if he were a sleeping babe. "How we have loved you. You've given us so much. Your laughter has been our courage. 'Hail Mary, full of grace . . . Holy Mary, Mother of God, pray for us now and on the day of our death.'"

"'Pray for us sinners.'" She'd left that out. Damienne kept talking softly, sweetly; every word was a song of praise, a prayer of gratitude, a blessing for my darling. I choked and sobbed, my heart hot with anger.

We wrapped him in the finest of my linen sheets. I wouldn't let Damienne sew it closed.

"Now we dig," said Damienne.

Tears poured down her face, yet she was calm and it infuriated me.

"Don't you care that he's dead?" I screamed. "How can you accept this?"

"I can't," she said. "But I have to do what must be done for Pierre."

That silenced me.

We started to dig between the house and the rocks in a sheltered spot. I wanted him as close to me as possible. We had no shovels. Damienne used the soup ladle and I a silver goblet. We hacked at tree roots with the axe and tore them out until our callused hands bled. We worked without pausing to breathe.

Birds sang. The sun rose high, warming the cool air. Some of the trees shook down leaves of gold, russet, and brilliant scarlet. Nature mocked our grief. The island was smiling on our misery.

"Evil!" I screamed, pulling stones from the earth and throwing them at the birds. All day I cursed and ripped at the earth with our feeble tools and my bare hands.

"Monstrous Eden! Foul murder!" I'd thought the demons were gone, vanquished by goodness and faith. More fool I!

"Stop," said Damienne.

"I won't stop," I shouted. "I'll tell the demons what I think. I'll—"

"It's deep enough," she said.

"Oh."

We'd dug down several feet, the length and width of a man. We pushed and pulled each other out of the grave and collapsed next to it.

"Damienne," I cried in her arms. "I can't bear it."

She cried with me and rocked me. "We must clean ourselves. We are too dirty to touch him."

I let her lead me to the stream. We threw off our heavy clothes and waded into the icy water in our shifts. I hardly noticed the cold, my raw hands, my aching back. My heart's anger and grief were chilling into numbness. I sank under the water. How easy it would be to stay in this cold death and join my Pierre. No. My lungs fought for air, and I broke the surface, gasping.

Dirt, caked blood, tears, and sweat washed away. I came out of the stream clean and calmer. We put on our less dirty clothes and sat on the bed by Pierre.

"Are you ready to say goodbye?" asked Damienne.

"No."

"Will you pray with me?"

"Yes."

"Our Father who art in heaven"—I said the words mechanically—"thy will be done on earth as it is in heaven."

Could this have anything to do with His will? "Forgive us our sins as we forgive those who sin against us." Never. I would never forgive this crime.

"Deliver us from evil . . . the power and the glory are yours, now and . . ."

God had no power here. This was Satan's realm.

". . . Forever. Amen," said Damienne.

She looked at me and I nodded. He was still—peaceful. I leaned over and kissed my love's cold lips. Already he smelled of death. I looked on him once more, my Pierre— no longer mine.

Weeping together, Damienne and I sewed his shroud closed.

As strong as we'd become from our incessant work on the island, it was a struggle to carry the dead weight of him.

We lay flat on the dirt, by the grave, to lower him into it.

"Speak," said Damienne.

"I can't."

"Try."

"I—"

"Tell him goodbye."

"Never."

"Tell him you love him."

"I love you, Pierre."

"Amen," said Damienne. She took a handful of dirt and threw it on him. "Now you."

Oh. I couldn't.

"If we don't put him safely in the ground, the scavengers will get him," she said.

So I worked with her, piling dirt on top of Pierre. Then we built a mound of stones over him. Damienne bound twigs into a cross and planted it in the stones, at my love's head.

Night fell. A fox barked. An owl flew overhead. A rabbit cried. Damienne brought me into our house, and we barred the door.

We sat together on the bed that had been Pierre's and mine.

My love was in the ground. And I lived, whether I would or not.

FOURTEEN

～

MORNINGS WERE THE WORST TIMES. ALL NIGHT long I'd dream of Pierre, his hands warm on me. We were together in the meadows and orchards of Montron and d'Arry. I smelled him, and it was his own true salty scent as well as that of baking bread and newly mown hay. Usually we were alone, although sometimes Isabeau, Maman, or Pierre's smiling mother and sisters appeared.

Pierre would kiss me.

"Don't," I'd say. "They'll see."

"They are happy for us, look."

Indeed, each of my dream visitors smiled warmly, pleased for our happiness and pleasure. We were in Eden, at last.

He was always merry, my Pierre, his whole face wrinkled in a grin, laughing out loud. Occasionally I laughed with him, but even in the sweetest of my dreams, I sensed that sorrow waited.

Waking startled and confused, I'd sit up and realize that I'd left the dream for the living nightmare. A river of grief poured out of me. Though it seemed there simply couldn't be any more tears, there always were.

"Why did he die?" I asked. "It seemed as if he'd gotten over the sickness, and then he died."

"I've gone over this many times," said Damienne. "I think he was poisoned by a mushroom. The sickness seems to pass, then comes swift death."

"Was there anything we could have done for him?"

"Certain mushrooms are deadly. There was nothing we could have done."

For a week we did little more than sit by Pierre's grave from waking to sleeping. We fed the fire and filled the cook pot with water from the stream. I wouldn't go with Damienne to look for food in the fields, nor would I let her leave me alone.

At dusk, Damienne set the pot on the fire and filled it with water and a few pieces of smoked meat. I had trouble chewing and swallowing the meat, no matter how long it had stewed. I could barely drink the broth but forced myself under Damienne's anxious eyes.

Damienne continued to mark the days on Pierre's calendar. She prayed continually throughout the day and perhaps the night. Morning and evening she coaxed me into joining her. The words came from my mouth but not my heart. We were so far away from any life we'd known. I wondered if we'd gone beyond God's reach. Perhaps He couldn't hear us from this wild land.

The days grew cool, and the nights cold. Leaves turned fantastic colors, unlike anything I'd ever seen in France. Such brilliant colors seemed diabolical. I would have blamed it on the island's demons, except that I could see the same profusion of color on the mainland. Perhaps the entirety of this vast new world was possessed.

Once a day I left Pierre's grave and climbed to the top of Mont Blanc to look out at the gulf and the immense forest rising on either shore. While Pierre lived, my world had been full; my rock had supported me. Now I looked out from my perch and was stunned by loneliness. I'd hardly noticed the huge emptiness around us. I knew that in the east were the fishing boats at Saint-Jean. Somewhere in the west, my uncle had planted his colony. Miles from either of them, we were the only ones living under this part of the endless sky. Not even natives lived here. I hardly ever saw the curls of smoke that showed from a native camp, and then they were always far in the distance. I certainly didn't long for native neighbors, but it was shocking to be so completely isolated.

On waking the eighth day after Pierre's death, when I went to sit and weep by his grave, Damienne stopped me.

"Today we must hunt," she said.

"No."

"Yes."

"I can't do that. I can't do anything," I said.

"You can. And you will."

"But—"

"Didn't you promise me that you wouldn't leave me alone?" She looked almost as stern as Father.

"I did promise, and I won't leave you." I answered like a guilty child, because I was guilty of wanting to die.

"By sitting, weeping, and not eating, you are calling to death, Marguerite. Death will hear you and surely come."

"Just a few more days, please?"

"Didn't you also promise Isabeau that you'd come back for her?"

"Yes." I couldn't look her in the eye.

Swear it, Isabeau had demanded, and I'd sworn it on my heart.

"For shame, Marguerite. You can reclaim your sister only if you live."

I didn't see how I'd keep my promise to Isabeau anyway, yet slipping into death would be a coward's way out.

"All right," I said and stood.

Silently we collected what we'd need for the day. We brought both guns, loaded and with extra bags of shot. Neither of us said it, but without Pierre we'd have to defend ourselves against savage men or beasts.

The day was leaden gray, heavy with the threat of rain. The woods seemed unnaturally quiet; no birds chirped, no squirrels chattered. With the cool weather, the mosquitoes had gone. There was a light wind, creating an insistent whisper against us in the dry and rustling leaves and the sighing pines. Damienne's hands shook as she set the snares. She had become nearly as awkward at it as I was. Twice the fragile contraptions broke and had to be reworked.

"You feel it, don't you?" I said.

"I feel nothing but my own clumsiness."

"It's the island, the d—"

"Marguerite, please, not the demons," she said. "Our life will be difficult enough now. Leave the demons out of it."

Damienne set four of the eight snares we'd brought and seemed exhausted by it.

"Let's go to the pond and see if the birds have missed any grapes," she said.

I agreed to anything to get us out of the deep woods. We'd only been to the grapevines by the pond on the eastern end of the island twice before. Pierre had ranged over the entire island almost daily; we'd usually stayed closer to our home fire. Perhaps Damienne was now trying to assert our claim to it all. She looked determined but was clearly frightened.

By the pond, gathering the last of the shriveled grapes, Damienne regained her composure. Away from the deep woods, the island's menace lessened.

"We must wash our clothes," said Damienne while we picked. "Soon the filth in them will rot the cloth. We've got to husband what little we have."

Husband! What a word to use. Without my husband what use was there to husband anything?

"I'm frightened, Marguerite," she said.

I stood still, staring at her, unable to even pretend to pick the grapes. Damienne had never before admitted fear.

"I miss Pierre so much," she said, "it frightens me."

Pierre was mine. *My Pierre.* How could she talk of missing him?

"Don't look at me that way, Marguerite. He was your husband, my friend, and *our* salvation."

Of course she was right. I didn't own him, although I was selfish enough to think so.

"I loved him dearly. Yet in the end, I failed him, and it torments me."

I couldn't bear to hear Damienne say such things. She was strong, and I was weak. If she stopped being strong and became plagued by fears and uncertainty, what would become of us?

"How could you have failed him?" I asked, trying to keep the terror out of my voice. "You told me there was no cure for him."

"I couldn't have saved his life, of that I am sure."

"Then what do you mean?"

"Pierre died unshriven. He didn't repent of his sins and gain forgiveness. It sits like lead on my heart."

"But we thought he was better. The sickness had passed and he was going to be well," I said. "Besides, Pierre was without sin."

"Marguerite, we all sin," said Damienne. "Didn't your father teach you anything?"

She spoke seriously, from the heart of her sorrow and

worry. What she said, on its own, wasn't a bit funny. But since all my father had ever taught me was about sin, it struck me. I began to laugh, a small nervous giggle.

Damienne glared at me.

"Sin is not funny."

"Of course not," I said, laughing harder.

Something was exploding inside me, and it came out as this insane laughter. The odd thing was that Damienne got caught in it, too. One moment she was looking at me sternly, the next she was choking with laughter. We collapsed on the ground, both of us hysterical. Tears came, and still we laughed. It ended finally in sobs. Then silence.

"Ah," said Damienne, wiping her eyes. "That was a gift from Pierre."

"Yes," I said. Laughter always came from Pierre. I felt calm. I'd crossed a bridge taking me from life before his death to the eternity of life after it. I was as desolate as before but could now accept living in the aftertime.

We picked up our basket and went back to the woods to check our snares. One fat rabbit and a noisy squirrel awaited us. Damienne killed the squirrel, and I the rabbit, smashing its head with a rock.

Back at our house, we gutted and cooked our prey. I ate the roasted meat without choking. Later I washed my face in the icy stream, the first time I'd cleaned myself since we'd buried Pierre. I sat by his grave. Damienne joined me. Together we prayed for his soul.

The next day we washed our linen, our bedding, and even the heavy woolen clothes, muddying the stream with our filth. It took most of the day and was hard, cold, heavy work. At least the sun worked for us, drying most everything by nightfall. We fell into sleep tired and peaceful.

We woke to cold unlike anything I'd ever known. The stream had frozen, and snow fell in a thick curtain. It was only mid-October.

"Is it winter already?" asked Damienne.

If it was, I didn't see how we could survive it. We couldn't hunt, fish, or gather firewood in this weather. We had stores to last a month, or two if we ate very little. And then—then what?

FIFTEEN

Mercifully, that first snowfall soon melted. We began a frantic effort to provision ourselves while the warmer weather held. Fear drove us. Damienne and I set snares and traps all over the island, concentrating on the smaller animals. A deer would have yielded more meat and hide, but managing a heavy carcass might have proven beyond just the two of us.

Alone.

Every task without Pierre was heavy with loneliness and twice as difficult and frightening. His confidence had lifted us above despair. Now we waded through its depths with every step we took.

We collected nuts, lugging them home in sacks made of our aprons. We dumped them in a corner of our house and raced back to the woods for more. When it seemed that we'd emptied the forest floor, Damienne climbed into the trees and shook down more nuts.

Perhaps the approaching winter was making the animals more frantic, too, and careless. Our traps and snares filled by the end of each day. We became expert at gutting and skinning the little creatures. Within a fortnight the outside walls of our house and beehive stores were covered with stretched and drying skins. The spinach and onions we'd planted yielded a scant bushel. It wasn't enough to make a big difference in our food stores, yet it would bring the flavor of home to our soups throughout the winter. We braided the onions and hung the garland we'd made by the hearth. We dried bouquets of spinach and hung those from our rough ceiling.

We needed more firewood than was imaginable. What we really needed were oak logs like the massive chunks of trees that the peasants hauled on sledges to burn in the great hearth of the hall at Montron.

There were plenty of trees here, but no heavy ax to fell them, saw to cut them, peasants to carry them, and no great hearth or hall, only our small fireplace in our sad hovel. We cut down and carried the biggest trees we could manage, slender saplings that would burn too quickly. We cut and stacked them between the beehives and our house.

"The wood makes a sort of stockade for us," said Damienne.

"Aye." Anything that put a margin of distance between us and the wild was welcome.

We worked so furiously we barely ate, and we fell into bed at dusk, too tired, hungry, and cold to carry on another minute. We wept in each other's arms and woke to begin work again.

Damienne had lost all of her roundness. Once well-hidden bones stood out on her face and body. Having started out bony, I must have become quite the scarecrow. I was glad not to have a looking glass. Our skin was browned and toughened by the sun and wind. My hands were too callused to feel my face. Looking at Damienne's face, the twin of my own ravagement, I knew it was leathery.

"Do you think we'll ever get back to France?" I mused one night when we were tucked into our bed with both cloaks over us.

"I do not think," said Damienne. "I only hope and pray."

"And if we can get back, what will we do? We can't go back to Montron. Father will have heard that we were sent off the ship in disgrace."

"We won't go to Montron," said Damienne. "We'll go to your aunt Clemence and beg her to take us in."

"But will she?"

"You aren't the first girl in the world who has sinned," said Damienne. "Your aunt will take you for your mother's sake and because she's never liked your father, and she will have grown to love Isabeau, who will beg for you."

"Damienne, I don't want to wait to be rescued."

"No, we can't wait," she said. "We will build a boat to take us to Saint-Jean."

She said it as if that had always been her plan, as if I hadn't begged for that very same thing over and over, only to be put off.

"But you never—" I began, feeling hot anger against her.

"That was before Pierre died," she said. "Then I worried that evil might befall him, and us, in Saint-Jean, that your uncle's wrath would reach us there."

"And now?"

"Two wretched women will receive pity, not scorn."

"And there's no possibility of us surviving here on our own," I said.

Damienne nodded.

That night, the first of November, it began to snow. When we woke, the world around us was silent, muffled by a thick blanket of snow. Throughout the day it snowed, into the night, and all the next day. We made forays to get water, having to break the ice to do so. We fetched wood for our hearth and tended the fire in the smokehouse. We put on our long woolen skirts for warmth, but they dragged in the drifting snow, making the slightest task heavy and difficult.

"I think we will now come to breeches," said Damienne. "May your sainted mother forgive me."

"Maman never saw snow like this," I said.

Mostly we sat by the fire sipping hot broth, trying to get warm. I was uncommonly tired and suffering from a stomach malady. Broth was the only thing that went down and stayed down.

"If only I had some pennyroyal and vinegar," said Damienne, fussing around me. "I could cure you."

"I'm not very ill, only tired," I said.

We both slept through the greater part of the day. In sleep I found Pierre. In my dreams I was not tired; I was beautiful and happy. My hair flowed down my back like brown silk. My arms were round and fair. I craved sleep, wanting to live in the happy place where I could forget winter and death.

The third day we woke to blinding sunshine—evil sun teasing us with its brightness and no heat.

There was no more hunting. We were too clumsy in our skirts to go into the woods. We broke holes in the ice and fished in our stream, catching barely enough to justify freezing on the frozen river. My stomach sickness seemed to ebb and flow. I ate heartily when it let me and fasted when it didn't.

We began planning our boat, neither of us knowing anything about it.

"The wild men make boats out of saplings and birch bark," said Damienne.

"And how do you know that?"

"Pierre heard it from the sailors and told me."

"There are birches nearby," said Damienne. "Let's try to strip them of their bark."

It was easier said than done. After a day of suffering in the cold by the birch grove, we came away with only two pieces intact, perhaps big enough to cover a bread basket.

"We'll try again," said Damienne, "on a warmer day."

There were no warmer days.

We experimented with what we had, soaking sticks until they were pliable, tying them together to form the framework of a miniature boat. Then we wet the birch bark and stretched it over the frame, sewing it onto the framework with thin strips of deer hide. It almost resembled a boat, a very leaky little boat.

We let it be and worked on the small animal pelts, shaping and rubbing them into softness with our benumbed hands. We pieced them together and sewed them into our cloaks, which we wore all day and slept under at night.

Damienne took sick with a cold. She had a slight fever but was left with a lingering cough. Her coughing woke me throughout the night, though she did her best to stifle it. I brewed an infusion of mint leaves and wished for honey.

Once I caught her leaving the house at midnight when a coughing fit was on her.

"Don't be insane!" I said.

"I just need some fresh air," she gasped.

"I quite realize how much our little hovel stinks," I said. "But that is not reason enough to freeze to death."

"You're right, though I am suffocating in here."

"Perhaps tomorrow we can open a window," I said, bundling her back in the bed and rubbing warmth into her icy hands.

"Aye, a window!"

It snowed every other day. Sometimes it came in great

swirling storms of howling wind and cracking thunder. Once I seemed to hear my father's voice in the wind: *Marguerite, repent your sin!*

What was my sin? Was it in loving Pierre too much, or too little?

After each new snowfall we stamped down paths from our door to the woodpile, the smokehouse, our stores, the stream, and back again. The snow was two feet deep at our doorstep. We had to crawl out so as not to bang our heads. The walls of snow hemmed us in, smothering us.

"Let's climb to the top of Mont Blanc," I said one clear day. "We need to see beyond our noses."

We reached the top, huffing and puffing like old women. It was worth it to see the great gulf stretching out before us. Ice grew out from its shores, leaving a wide channel of dark roiling water. Stark dark and white replaced autumn's fantastic colors. The sky was everything now. Wispy clouds like angel's wings flew overhead and into the horizon.

"It was a beautiful wedding," said Damienne.

"Yes, 'twas beautiful. We married at the top of the world."

Damienne drew close to me. "At least you had him for a time."

At least. Now it seemed such a small piece of time.

"Look!" said Damienne. "What's that?"

Lumbering up from the shore near First Fire, came something large and furred.

"A bear?"

"I don't know. Let's go back and load our guns."

We skidded down the rocks and made our way as quickly as we could to our house.

Six braves were there before us, crammed into our house, and picking over our things. Seeing them, we backed out of the doorway.

"Should we run?" whispered Damienne.

"We've nowhere to go," I said. "Besides, they would catch us. We'll give them presents and hope that they go."

"What if they don't?"

It was a chilling question.

I heard noise behind me and whirled around to see the "bear" crossing our frozen stream. Only it wasn't a bear but the native leader who'd come in the summer, now wearing an entire bearskin. I stifled a cry and fell into a curtsy to cover my fright and confusion. Damienne dropped beside me.

I rose unsteadily, with as much dignity as I could muster.

"Welcome," I said, trying my best to sound calm.

The leader nodded and spoke some words. I stood aside from the door, inviting him in.

Damienne took my shaking hand in hers, and we followed after him.

"Lord help us," she said.

"Amen."

SIXTEEN

～

THE NATIVES CROWDED INTO LA MAISON.
They reeked of the skins they wore and of the rancid fat
gleaming on their black hair, reflecting the fire's glow. We
might well have been entertaining bears. My stomach heaved,
and I fought hard against the surge of nausea and fear. Damienne and I held tightly to each other. I could feel her heart
racing in time with my own.

The men ignored us, intent on examining our few things.
They spoke little. I couldn't catch even the sounds of their
words, which seemed more like low growling than speech.

Men, I thought, trying to calm myself. *These are men, not
beasts, different from Frenchmen, yet only men.* Oh, but to face
them without Pierre. Had they already guessed that he was
no longer here to defend us?

One of them picked up the odd little boat we'd made. He

showed it to the others. They turned it this way and that, then burst into laughter.

"Boat," I said and shocked myself with the strength of my own voice.

"*Canu,*" said the leader.

"*Canu,*" I repeated. "We want *canu.*"

He looked at me, his black eyes curious. How could I make him understand? I went to the open chest where two of the men were pawing through our things. I pushed them aside. Truly I don't know from whence came my recklessness.

I pulled out my silver goblets and brought them to the leader. I put one in his hand and the rest at his feet.

"*Canu,*" I said. "Bring me a *canu.*" I opened my arms wide to show him how big it should be and pointed to Damienne. "*Canu.*" Tears were threatening. I couldn't cry. I was bargaining, not begging.

The leader said something, and his men handed him one of our guns. He held the gun and looked at me.

"*Canu,*" he said.

I looked at Damienne, and she nodded.

Yes, we would give one gun for a chance to escape.

I nodded.

They could take the gun, anyway. They could take everything if they wished. They could take us and eat us, if the tales were true. What could we do to stop them? Nothing. But they weren't beasts, they were men.

"Damienne, get food from our stores," I said. "We've got to feed them."

"Are you sure?"

I hated to part with a morsel, but knew we had to offer them food.

"Yes."

She went and quickly returned with smoked hare, grouse, and roasted nuts. We gave food first to the leader and set the rest on our brick hearth. The men sat down and ate.

One of the natives kept his eye on Damienne, the same man who'd wanted to take her last summer. Eventually, he stood up and came to the corner by the door where we huddled. Damienne was shaking terribly. He pulled her arm out from under her cloak. She shut her eyes and frantically murmured prayers,

"Hail Mary, Holy Mother, help me. Save me. Hail Mary, Holy Mother..."

The native pinched her thin wrist. He pulled at her hair, short and matted like mine. He shook his head and said something that sounded sad. She was too much changed for the worse; he didn't want her anymore.

When the wild men left, Damienne and I barred the door and collapsed against each other.

"Lord, we've been spared," said Damienne.

"Spared," I said and began laughing hysterically.

"Please, stop," said Damienne. "Marguerite, please."

The fear I'd been stifling came rushing out in mad laughter and tears.

"We've...we've had *les sauvages* to dinner," I managed finally.

"And they could have had us *for* dinner," she said.

I nodded. And with one last shuddering sob I calmed down.

"Do you think they've left the island?" Her eyes were still wide with fear.

"I think they come here only to hunt." They probably feared the demons as much as I did.

"Do you think they knew Pierre was gone?" she asked.

"Of course they knew," I said. "Look at us, two frozen sticks without enough dignity to run a comb through our hair."

Damienne stepped back and took a good, long look at me.

"Now I don't know whether to laugh or cry," she said. "Do I look as bad as you?"

"Yes," I said, "perhaps a bit worse."

"Then I needn't worry about the native coming back for me."

"No, that won't be a worry."

"I'll comb through your hair," said Damienne, "if you'll do mine."

"With pleasure."

We spent the next hour or so tending to each other, soothing our fears in the simple act of grooming. Once more I got out the sewing scissors to cut off the snarls and matted parts too tangled to comb out. Then we heated water on the fire and washed our heads. We stripped down and washed our bodies. I'd never before been shy with Damienne. Unaccountably, now I was. I didn't want her to see me, scrawny and shrunken, with strangely swollen breasts. I turned away from her, and she from me.

Once clean, we put on fresh shifts and threw the dirty ones into the kettle to boil away the dirt and sour smell of our bodies.

Shivering, we climbed into bed under our cloaks and covers. It wasn't yet night, but we were done in.

"Do you think the wild men will bring us a boat?" asked Damienne.

"Do you?"

"I'm sure they understood you, and you certainly paid them well enough, but..." Damienne's voice trailed off.

"We won't know until they return."

"If they return."

"Aye. I wish they'd given us some more of their bread," I said.

"Or another deer," said Damienne.

"While we are wishing," I said, "let us wish for salvation."

"That I do constantly."

We were silent for a time. The heaviness of sleep was pulling me along.

Damienne whispered in my ear, "You spoke up like a man today, Marguerite."

"Father said many times that it was unseemly for a maiden to speak in the presence of men."

"We are far from France and the world of your father."

"Aye."

"You were brave, Marguerite. I could never have faced those men as you did."

"Is desperation courage?"

Damienne sighed. "We are both desperate; you spoke up and won the leader's admiration."

"I think they pitied us," I said.

"That, too."

During the night, fierce winds tore across the island, shrieking horribly. I woke several times, feeling the demons' anger. I did something I usually left to Damienne. I prayed. Either the winds abated or the "Our Father" blocked out their noise. I fell asleep praying and slept peacefully until morning.

SEVENTEEN

～

THE COLD HURT. IT BURNED. MOST OF THE TIME we huddled in our hovel, by the smoking fire. Long days passed with the two of us wrapped in our cloaks, shivering.

"Isn't it warmer today?" said Damienne, her teeth chattering.

"Indeed, it is almost balmy."

In this way we tried to fool ourselves into a warm thought.

Several times a day need sent us out into the biting cold. We had to get food from our stores. We had to break the ice of the stream to get water and wrench firewood from the snow-bound piles. Setting new traps or snares was impossible; our frozen fingers simply couldn't manage it.

Never had I seen such snow. Mounds of snow hid bushes and shrubs. Snow smothered rock, trail, and stream, everything but the sounding sea. Snow sucked the color out of the world, reducing sky and sea to milky gray.

When it wasn't storming, we went as far as the woods, wearing breeches we'd pieced together from small pelts, the fur against our skin. We tried to stamp down a trail, but each new snowfall defeated us. Sometimes the frozen crust of snow was strong enough to bear our weight. Then we went into the deep wood to collect fallen branches. There was no lack of wood. What we lacked was the strength to carry it.

We piled wood on a sledge we'd made by lashing branches together, tied ourselves to the sledge with vines, and pulled together like a team of oxen.

"All we need is a yoke," said Damienne.

"Is that all we need?"

"Yes," said Damienne. "If only we had a yoke, our lives would be complete."

We laughed. We laughed at almost anything in those dark days. It wasn't the joyful laughter we'd shared with Pierre. This was grim stuff, but better than tears.

Damienne's cough persisted throughout the day and worsened at night. I tried to make her stay inside while I got wood, but she always came with me, though the cold must have harmed her. I couldn't blame her for needing to get out of our stinking, dark box. And though I wanted to spare her, I needed her near me. Being alone even for a short time was unbearable. Together we kept the demons at bay, except at night, when they laughed and howled around our house.

"It's just the wind," said Damienne as she shivered, coughed, and burrowed closer to my small warmth.

"Aye, the wind," I said. And let it be the wind, and not my demons, teasing us, setting us on edge, stealing what little peace we might hope for. What was the point of arguing? It was better if one of us didn't believe in the evil here.

"It is already mid-December," said Damienne, marking the doorpost one morning.

"Already?" I said, thinking of the horrible eternity of our time here. Damienne's coughing woke me continually throughout the night. I'd have just begun to dream of Pierre in the sunlit meadows of Montron when I'd be wrenched back to my awful loneliness by her cough.

We drank broth all day long, to fill our bellies and warm us. We ate sparingly, being careful with our stores. Every time I went to get us a few strips of meat, I tried to calculate how much remained, how many days it would feed us, and how many more days of this frozen hell we'd have to face.

I was plagued by hunger. Even when we'd just eaten, and I should have been content, my stomach whined for more food.

Our monthlies had stopped with the onset of winter.

"Perhaps it's the cold," said Damienne, "or our diet."

"At least we're spared the bother of washing our bloodied rags."

"Yes," said Damienne, looking at me sharply. "Although there are other bothers."

"What is that supposed to mean?"

"Nothing. How are you feeling?"

"Cold, hungry, tired, the usual."

"Has your stomach settled?"

"Mostly, yes."

Damienne nodded. She had a look I couldn't quite fathom. What was she getting at? I would have quizzed her, only she was beset by a coughing fit.

"Christmas is almost here," said Damienne on a dark morning.

A snowstorm raged outside, holding us captive by the fire. The demons raged as they did on the blackest, coldest nights.

"It is little to me," I said. "You know we never celebrated Christmas at Montron. Father said it was pagan."

"I know," she said. "But my family always kept Christmas. So I did, too, even at Montron."

"You never told me, and how could you without my knowing? Why didn't you tell me?"

"Had I told you, your father would have found out and used it to get rid of me."

"I wouldn't have told him."

"No, but your brothers were always spying on you. They would have been glad to tell him such a thing."

I was only a little satisfied. I didn't think Damienne had ever held anything secret from me.

"Tell me what you did to keep Christmas."

"I made gifts that Pierre carried to my family each year,"

she said. "And your mother always sent me on some errand to d'Arry at Christmas so that I could go to Mass and sing 'Joyeux Noël.'"

"Oh."

We fell silent.

Outside, the demons battered our house and roared. Next to Maman and Pierre, Damienne was the safest harbor I knew. I didn't like her having secrets. The demons seemed to revel in this small breach between us. They shook the house and blew the smoke back down the chimney into our faces.

"The wind frightens me today," said Damienne. "Marguerite."

"Yes."

"Please read to me the story of Christ's birth."

"If you wish."

"Yes, please."

I went to the chest and took out Maman's Holy Gospel.

"Read from Saint Luke," said Damienne. "Begin with the angel Gabriel."

I'd heard the story of the Annunciation many times. Yet the words felt new to me as I read them to Damienne, perhaps because I'd always heard them in the pastor's drone or Father's thundering voice. Perhaps reading the Gospel in this wild place, haunted by evil spirits, gave the story a whole new meaning.

"'The angel Gabriel was sent to . . . Nazareth, to a virgin. . . . The virgin's name was Mary.'"

He called her blessed.

"'Do not be afraid, Mary. . . . You will conceive and bear a son, and you will name him Jesus.'"

"Listen," said Damienne.

I put down the book. The winds had quieted; the demons no longer roared.

"The Gospel defeats them," said Damienne.

"What?"

"God's word is stronger than your demons," said Damienne. "See how He has hushed them."

"But you don't believe in my demons," I said.

"It isn't wise to name the evil spirits. It gives them strength. It's best to save your thoughts for the *Bon Dieu.*"

"Does that mean that I've been helping the evil?"

"Evil will help itself," she said.

"And I could better resist it."

"Just don't give evil any room in your heart," said Damienne. "Please keep reading."

"'How can this be, since I am a virgin?'

"'The angel said to her, The Holy Spirit will come upon you.'"

Mary seemed to accept everything so calmly. I think I would have had a few more questions for that angel. I felt a flutter in my stomach and hoped it didn't bode more sickness. I needed to catch my breath.

"Damienne, do you suppose Mary looked more like dark Berthe or fair Claudine?"

"She might have resembled someone we know," Damienne said. "And yet—"

"What about one of the Maries?"

"No. The Maries are sweet, but Mary was made of stronger stuff," said Damienne. "I wonder how they are faring."

"Better than us," I said. "They have men to hunt for meat and to protect them. There still must be plenty of food in the ships' stores. They will have built strong, warm houses with stone chimneys, and have raging fires to warm them. And—"

"It will be snowing as hard wherever they are as it is here."

"Yes."

"Perhaps they are also beset by demons."

"Berthe, Claudine, and the Maries have my uncle and the pastor. They don't need demons."

"Marguerite! For shame," said Damienne, but she couldn't help laughing. "Read some more."

I read about Mary visiting her cousin Elizabeth.

"Perhaps Mary looked like Isabeau," I said.

"Isabeau is still a baby," said Damienne. "I can't picture her as the mother of God. I think the Virgin looked like you."

"Don't be ridiculous."

That night a new noise woke me. Something about it wrenched me from sleep and brought me bolt upright. Someone, or something, banged against our door. It was neither the wind nor my imagination. Something big, solid, and real was trying to break into our house. I pulled on my boots and loaded the harquebus with shaking hands. Damienne slept on. I stood before the door, ready to shoot if the branch barring our door broke and this something burst in.

The door held, the banging ceased, and whatever it was moved off. I went to the door and listened. The night was windless and oddly still. I heard it attack our storehouse. That door had only a simple latch. It could easily break in and steal our food. Our precious food.

"What is it?" asked Damienne, roused from sleep as I pulled my cloak off the bed and around me.

"*Shh,* I don't know. But I must see."

"Marguerite!"

Before she could stop me, I drew the bar and opened the door. A half-moon lit the night enough to see clearly. Blue shadows fell across the snow-covered world, deepening to blackness. A few feet in front of me stood what looked like the native leader in his bearskin cloak. Except that this bearskin was as pale as the snow. I didn't know whether to greet him or remain still. Perhaps this was a different native, one who had come to harm us. Yet I couldn't shoot without knowing. My fingers were already numb with cold. If I had to, would I be able to shoot?

I aimed the gun and spoke. "Who are you?"

My voice rent the night stillness. The bear shape swung around to face me. I squinted to find the man's face hidden in the bear's fur. There was no man, only bear. A huge white bear snarling. One lunge and he'd be on top of me.

I heard Pierre's voice inside my head, saying, *Steady*. I held my breath. *Aim. Fire!*

I pulled the trigger, and the gun exploded.

The bear fell.

I dropped the gun and screamed.

"Mon Dieu!" shouted Damienne. She ran to my side. "You've killed a bear!"

I was shaking. "I killed a bear!" My voice echoed back to me. "Is it really dead?"

Damienne got close enough to poke the carcass. "Dead," she said. "Shot through the heart."

I hugged Damienne and swung her around. "A bear, I've killed a bear."

It became a dance of victory. Round and round we went, laughing and whooping like savages. We stopped to catch our breath and gloat over the dead bear.

"Bien!" said Damienne. "Now we have work to do."

We had to skin the bear and cut up the carcass before it froze. We built a raging fire nearby to warm us and light our work.

"What a huge brute," said Damienne. "He will be food for weeks."

There was no need for the laborious process of drying and smoking the meat. We'd leave it in one of our beehives without fire, and it would keep frozen until spring.

"And he will keep us warm," said Damienne.

"Aye."

We struggled with the monster. He was so heavy, and we so weak. But triumph gave us strength and ingenuity. We used thick branches as levers to move him. And once he was gutted, we managed fairly well. Still it was nasty, bloody work all through the night, and well into the next day.

When the meat was safely stored and the skin scraped, stretched, and pegged along the north wall of our house, we sat by our hearth eating a great chunk of the pungent roasted meat, its fat dripping down our chins.

"Pas mal," I said. "Not beef, but not bad."

"Pierre would be proud of you," said Damienne.

"He'd be astonished." I laughed because I could hear his delighted laughter.

"He came to help me," I said.

Damienne nodded. "He stood beside you."

"And steadied my aim and my arm."

Damienne crossed herself. "He saved us."

"Yes."

"The bear would have eaten everything, including us!"

"More may come from the mainland," I said and shivered.

"Then they will be sorry," said Damienne, laughing.

I tried to laugh with her but couldn't. Just because I'd killed this bear didn't mean that the next one wouldn't kill me.

EIGHTEEN

⁓

In late january, snowbound as we often were in those dark days, Damienne and I sat before the fire piecing skins into short jackets. Our cloaks were as cumbersome as our long skirts. We needed to keep warm and still be able to move freely.

"Remember sitting in the sun, shelling peas for Cook?" I asked. "Can you remember being warm?"

"No," said Damienne.

"Neither can I."

I began to sing songs Maman had taught us. Damienne joined in when she wasn't coughing. Our voices competed with the wailing winds. I was singing a lullaby Maman had crooned over Isabeau's cradle when I noticed that Damienne had stopped her sewing and had her eyes hard upon me.

"You're pregnant," she said.

"What?"

"You heard me."

"But I can't believe my ears."

"You haven't had your monthlies—"

"Neither have you," I said.

"Listen to me, Marguerite. Your breasts are swollen, your stomach grows though you eat little, and in this prison of winter you are blooming like a rose."

"Now you are imagining things," I said.

"You and Pierre made love many times, including his last night on earth," she said. "Why should a baby surprise you?"

"Because it's impossible to imagine a baby here."

A baby. The idea of a baby was a small fissure opening my heart.

"A baby!"

"This baby will bring Pierre back to us," said Damienne. "We must make sure he will be healthy and safe."

I felt my belly, tight and round. Something stirred. It was the faint flutter I'd felt and dismissed many times before. Was this moth inside me a baby?

"Of course," I said.

"You must eat more."

I nodded, hardly hearing her.

"You mustn't strain yourself."

"What?"

"You mustn't lift anything heavy—"

"Why not?"

"The baby, Marguerite. You could hurt the baby."

Terror quickly stole my instant of joy.

"I can't have a baby here!"

"You may have to," said Damienne.

"I'll die and the babe will, too."

"No. I'll help you. We'll manage all right."

"But—"

"I helped my mother with her last baby, and I helped your mother with Isabeau."

"Your mother came to help Maman," I said.

"Yes, and I helped her."

"And you saw everything that was done?"

"Everything."

"Why wasn't I there?"

"Because your mother wanted to spare you."

"Now I'm on this evil island with no help and no knowledge, and..." I started to weep, frightened for myself and my child.

Damienne didn't try to hush me. She let me grieve.

Tangled up with my fear was longing for Pierre and Maman. Like a babe myself, I wanted the comfort and safety of my mother's arms—not to be had again in this world.

The afternoon passed slowly. By nightfall, I'd just about cried myself empty. Damienne handed me a bowl of broth, skimmed over with bear fat and laden with stewed meat. I ate it willingly.

Winds buffeted *La Maison*. The demons' raucous cries began early that night. The island had taken Pierre. Now the demons had something equally precious to steal from me. Yet I felt the small tickle of hope inside me. Yes. I had something precious, and I'd not give it up. I'd not let them take my child.

"We've got to leave here," I said.

Damienne nodded. "Somehow we will leave here."

She knew as little as I how we would do that, but having her say it reassured me.

"Tell me about having this child," I said.

"It won't happen for months—not until late June, or even July."

"I want to be ready."

"You will," she said. "I will help you."

January dragged into February. Damienne grew thin as I thickened. A fever often possessed her late in the day. She tried to hide it from me, but I saw her flushed face and worried.

Yet with all my worries and fears about the future and the safety of the babe, I relished his presence. I felt the roll and lurch of him swimming in me. I was the babe's ocean and the ship carrying him. He was my love, living again.

Winter scarcity made the animals bolder and more stupid. Foxes and raccoons came often to get at our stores. I always heard them, but sometimes later rather than sooner, after they'd eaten our food. I'd kill the thief. Fox and raccoon made good pelts but poor eating. So, wearing our fur jackets and breeches, we ventured out to hunt and fish. The weakness and nausea of the early winter had left me. I was full of energy and strength. And the baby inside me threw off heat like a small stove. Damienne had no baby giving her heat and suffered terribly in the cold. I tried to go on my own, but she wouldn't allow it. We brought our sledge of woven branches to drag back firewood and game. On it was the bearskin and our fur-lined cloaks. When I saw Damienne turning blue and shivering, I'd sit her on the sledge and wrap us both in the cloaks. We'd chew some fatty strips of smoked venison, then I'd rub some of my warmth into her.

A great many snow-white ptarmigans flocked to our shore, near First Fire. We hunted them with a net we'd made out of a linen tablecloth. We had cut the cloth into reed-thin strips and braided the strips into ropelike lengths. Those, we'd tied and knotted into a net. We began clumsily, but soon we were capturing dozens of the poor stupid birds. We gutted, plucked, and packed them in snow with the remaining bear meat. Their feathers made us two plump pillows.

February neared its end. In France we'd be seeing signs of spring. Not here. Snow and cold continued as if the spring would never come.

Damienne and I huddled in our cloaks, ice fishing in the stream. A great stag came out of the woods near us to break the ice for a drink. Damienne and I had been quiet for some time, muffled in our furs, probably smelling more of rabbit than human. I stealthily reached for the harquebus that was always at my side, shed my heavy cloak, took aim, and fired. The stag lurched and fell.

"Bless you!" cried Damienne.

"Me or the stag?" I asked.

"Both of you," she said, laughing, "and the Holy Mother, who has sent us enough and more."

"Look, Pierre," I called. "I am a great hunter!"

But the laughter froze in my throat. Pierre was in the cold ground. He couldn't see anything.

"He is watching out for you," said Damienne, seeing my sorrow. "Try to believe that. You believe in evil, believe also in good."

"*Hmm.*" I couldn't answer her and remain dry eyed.

We skinned and gutted the stag where he'd fallen and turned the handsome beast into enough meat to see us through a month of eating.

"If ever we get back to France," I said, "I will fast as the nuns do and eat only bread, milk, cheese, fruits, and vegetables. I've had enough meat."

"*When* we get to France," said Damienne with a ferocity I'd never seen before. "Marguerite, have faith in this, because it must happen."

"I will try to believe," I said, wishing for her faith.

By the time we'd stored the carved meat and stretched and pegged the deerskin to the side of the house, we were both too exhausted to speak. We threw scraps of venison into the pot on the fire and sat before it, waiting for our well-earned dinner.

Damienne began to shiver terribly. I started to rub warmth into her and found her soaking wet under her furs.

"You've worked too hard," I said, helping her out of her wet garments and into dry clothes. I tried rubbing warmth into her. "You're ill and must rest."

"I'm all right," she said. "It will pass."

She started coughing. It racked her whole body and continued for many minutes. "What can I do?" I asked. It was horrid to be so helpless, to watch her suffer.

"N . . . nothing," she gasped.

I held her to me, trying to give her my strength. Her head rested on my chest, and the coughing began to lessen. It finally ceased. She sighed mightily and pulled away from me.

"Mon Dieu!" she said, looking aghast at my chest.

A bright red flower of blood blossomed where her head had rested. Not understanding at first, I felt to see if I was wounded. I was whole and well. It was Damienne's blood staining my bodice.

NINETEEN

I wouldn't let damienne come with me into the woods anymore, and she was too weak now to protest. Before I'd leave to hunt or gather firewood, I'd pile wood on the fire and stack an ample supply of branches nearby to keep it burning throughout the day. I filled the pot from the stream, and as I left, made her bar the door.

If she stayed quiet during the day, I'd find her almost looking well on my return. But if the demons troubled her or she overtired herself trying to clean or cook for us, then she'd be feverish and weak by evening. And I'd scold her.

"It's hard to remain idle all day."

"You must rest."

"Read to me, Marguerite. It's the only thing that settles my spirit."

And mine, too, I'd found.

Once I'd left her during the day and was on my own, my courage faltered. I'd press my belly and wait to feel the babe move. Feeling him with me made me braver than I actually was.

I often climbed Mont Blanc to look beyond our island prison. The gulf seemed frozen solid across to the near mainland shore. If it were summer, I'd risk that crossing. Of course in summer there wouldn't be ice to cross on. I wondered if the demons would let me go. It would be easy enough for them to crack the ice and drown me. Even if the demons didn't follow me across, the mainland would have many dangers. Most deadly would be the cold. We couldn't build a shelter in this weather. There'd be bears, wolves, more natives, different tribes who might not pity two women on their own, who might..."Stop it!" I shouted, and the wind laughed at me. I was frightening myself over mere supposing. Hunger was frightening enough, and I could fight that by catching a brace of ptarmigans for our dinner.

February dragged into March, and the merciless cold persisted. It was far too cold to clean ourselves or our linen, and La Maison stank worse than any animal pen I'd known. Snow lay deep on the ground, ice thick on the river and streams.

"The plows will be at work now in Montron," said Damienne.

"Aye." The slow, massive oxen would be yoked and pulling heavy plows through the resisting earth. Eating required so much work. I'd never considered the amount of labor necessary to feed us at Montron. The peasants worked all year, plowing, digging, sowing, weeding, and reaping, just to put bread on the table. And we ate much more than bread. Every bit of food on the groaning boards in the hall at Montron came from the ceaseless toil of many men and women.

"Read to me," said Damienne.

I read Matthew, Mark, Luke, and John so many times I could almost recite the texts.

"When you're gone during the day," said Damienne, "I say the verses that I remember. Still I like to hear you read. The words seem like old friends, always telling me something new."

"I'll teach you to read for yourself."

"No. I can't read," she said. "I'm too stupid to learn letters."

"Don't be silly," I said. "I can teach you."

"No. It isn't right," Damienne insisted. "I don't want to learn."

"But why?"

"If you teach me to read, no man will have me to wed."

"That's nonsense—" I began.

"You are high born. Reading may be all right for ladies, but not for me."

I was tempted to argue more, but it wouldn't have changed her mind. Considering how frail she looked, the strength of her opinions startled me.

"Very well, I will read, and you will listen."

I read from Matthew, how the two Marys went to the tomb to prepare Jesus' body for burial. And then came the angel, white as snow, bright as lightning, and rolled back the stone covering the tomb. The angel spoke gently to the Marys, bidding them tell the disciples that Jesus had risen from the dead, and they departed "'with fear and great joy—'"

"Mark tells it differently," said Damienne.

"Yes," I said and read the same passage in Mark. "His story ends with the fearful women running away."

"It still seems complete," she said.

"It does." I understood perfectly why Mark's Marys simply ran, too afraid to carry the news to anyone. "We're becoming biblical scholars," I said.

"No, that is only for men, churchmen," she said. "We are simply two women trying to keep our wits in a strange land."

That we were.

One night in late March we were woken by a hideous sound, so loud and horrible I thought the world was ending. Damienne and I clung to each other.

"What could it be?" she whispered.

An awful scream gave way to huge explosive cracks and booms, like thunder. It wasn't a storm, and no living thing could make a noise so great and terrible.

"Is it the Second Coming?" asked Damienne.

It did seem like something out of the warnings in the Book of John.

"Wouldn't we have seen other signs? And wasn't it to be continuous day at the end of the world? Here it is pitch-black night."

I wasn't ready for the world to end, not yet, not before I'd seen my baby born and grown into a fine strong man like his father.

The noise continued through the long night. Sometimes we dozed, exhausted by our fear, only to be thrown awake by another shattering *crack!*

When daylight showed through the chinks in our walls, Damienne and I ventured out to see what was left of our world. Warm sunlight blinded us. When our eyes adjusted to the brightness, everything seemed as it always had been. We stood quietly looking at a sunlit winter day not unlike many other days.

"Listen," I said, catching a sound, familiar yet fresh and wonderful.

Damienne concentrated, and soon her smile matched my own. "The stream," she said.

The stream was flowing.

"The thaw!" I said.

We had heard not the Apocalypse during the night but the ice breaking on the river. A season of hope was beginning.

The days grew warmer and longer. Snow still fell, but never very hard, and usually it turned to slushy rain. And we weren't ever buried in snow as we had been in January's blizzards. Damienne sat outside on sunny days and grew a bit stronger, although her cheeks remained hollow and her eyes enormous in her ravaged face.

Hunting in the woods was impossible. The soft wet snow and mud beneath it were as treacherous as quicksand. I went to the shore. The ptarmigans had departed with the coming of spring. I gathered seaweed and dug for shellfish at low tide. We ate the briny seaweed and rubbery clams and tried to laugh at how awful they tasted.

Spring came slowly, and winter held on with tenacity. The in-between sodden, brown, befogged world made us impatient and ill-tempered.

One morning in mid-April I climbed Mont Blanc to look out at the flowing water and made plans for finding food that day. Our stores were growing low. If we ate very little, there would be enough for a week, perhaps ten days. The growing baby hungered, as did I. What we needed was a deer, or one of the fat seals I could see frolicking in the river below. Perhaps I could lure one onshore with fish bait, then shoot it with the harquebus.

Something on the western horizon caught my attention. There seemed to be small patchy clouds. Not clouds! They were sails!

"Ships!" I cried. *"Ships!"* I ran, stumbling and tripping, back down to Damienne.

"Ships! Ships are coming from the west!" I shouted, startling her out of a doze in the sunshine.

"What! Ships? Oh!"

"They must be my uncle's ships. We must go down to the shore and build a big fire so that they can't miss us," I said. "They'll take us back, won't they?"

"Please, God, they will," said Damienne.

"They have to, don't they? Should I bring our chest to the shore?"

"No, it's too heavy," said Damienne. "Just bring the Gospel."

I ran into our house for Maman's book and looked quickly around. Was there anything else here I'd ever want to see again? I grabbed my skirt to cover my breeches and took the bearskin and my fur-lined cloak from the bed. What about Pierre? I'd have to leave him here alone. No. What had died would stay, and our love would come with me.

I rushed out the door. "Let's go quickly!"

"How near are the ships?" asked Damienne.

"Quite far, but—"

"Bring fire in the cook pot, and something to eat while we wait," she said.

As anxious as I was to get to the shore to hurry the ships to our salvation, I obeyed. We had to get quickly to the shore, and somehow get the ships to stop for us. Even if my uncle's heart was as hard as ever, surely one of the other captains would rescue us. To leave us here would be murder. How could a Christian pass us by?

We set out.

This was Damienne's greatest effort in many weeks. Soon she was gasping for air, trying to keep up with me. She couldn't possibly walk all the way to the shore.

I dropped everything I'd been carrying and wrapped the food in the bearskin.

"Get on my back," I said.

"You can't carry me."

"I can try."

"Marguerite, think of the babe."

"I am thinking of the babe. We have a chance to leave this place. We mustn't miss it."

She climbed on my back. I was shocked at how little she weighed, not much more than Isabeau. I hurried as much as I could. By the time we reached the shore, I was panting.

"Just as well it is downhill," I said, collapsing at the shoreline.

On flatter ground, without the wet snow to hinder her, Damienne could walk. I rested briefly, then clambered up a rise to check on the ships. They were still barely more than little squares of sails. I went back for our things, then wrapped Damienne securely in our furs. I collected driftwood and got a small fire started.

Soon I'd built quite a blaze, which sent up billows of smoke. They couldn't possibly not see it. I went back to the rise. The ships were no longer dots of sails but small, complete ships fast approaching. I ran back to Damienne.

"Sit beside me," she said.

"I must feed the fire."

I could not be still. I gathered more branches from the

edge of the forest, then ran back to check on the location and the progress of the ships. They were still some way off but coming steadily, surely straight at us.

"Marguerite, please," called Damienne.

I threw myself beside her, breathless from my frantic work.

"Read to me."

"Oh, I can't. I'm too worried."

"I am, too," she said. "And I can't bear to see you racing about. You'll harm your child."

"Very well."

"Eat something," she said.

"No, I'll choke."

"Put on your skirt and hide your belly."

I obeyed instantly. Carrying Pierre's child and wearing a man's clothes would only enrage my uncle, and I must try to pacify him.

"Now, please read to me." Damienne looked as anxious as I was. We both needed God's words.

I nodded and took the book from her.

"Read the Beatitudes."

"'Blessed are the poor in spirit.... Blessed are those who mourn.... Blessed are the meek.'"

We were meek, and my uncle was strong.

"'Blessed are the merciful.'"

"Will my uncle have mercy?"

"We must pray to the Holy Mother to soften his heart."

But would the Sieur de Roberval listen to a woman, even

the Holy Mother? I tried to pray and couldn't. The ships drew closer. The largest, the *Sainte-Anne,* came first.

I stayed by Damienne until I could make out figures on deck. Then I flew to the water's edge, waved my arms wildly, and shouted.

"Help us! Save us!"

More figures appeared on deck. Now I could distinguish sailors, *sieurs,* and women. Only two women were at the rail. My uncle would have them shut up in the horrid little cabin. If only Damienne and I could get back into that foul little hole.

"Please stop!" I begged.

All sails set, the ships labored through the water, ever nearer. Soon they'd be opposite us. A few more people gathered at the rails. I looked for Berthe and the golden curls of Claudine.

"Marie!" I screamed. "Marie!"

She waved to me, her face a mask of sorrow.

Faintly I heard her. "He won't stop...he..." The wind blew her words away from me. "...From Berthe."

Two sailors threw a sea chest over the rail, toward me.

I waded into the freezing water. The *Sainte-Anne* was only a few yards from me. The sails were full. The ship flew. "Stop!" I shouted. "Please!"

The *Sainte-Anne* came as close as it could get to the island. There was no sign of my uncle on deck.

"Berthe is dead," called Marie. "Claudine, dead... Giselle...Marie-Christine...Antoinette..."

"Give us a boat," I cried. "Please help us. Don't leave us here."

"All dead...Jeanne-Marie..." Her words carried faintly as the *Sainte-Anne* passed me.

"Please God!"

The second ship came quickly abreast of me.

"You must stop!" I shouted. Several sailors stood at the rail. One crossed himself.

"Marguerite," called Damienne from the shore. "Come back!"

I was up to my waist in the water. Any farther, and I'd be caught in the current. My legs were numb. I grabbed for the sea chest that floated near me. "Help!"

"He won't hear you," said Damienne. "Come back now, or the water will take you."

The third ship sailed past me, much farther from the shore.

"Marguerite!"

I turned and saw Damienne coming into the water after me. The water would kill her.

"Stop!" I called. "I'm coming. Get me the bearskin."

She left the water. I turned my back on the ships and dragged the sea chest toward the shore.

TWENTY

~

I PULLED MYSELF, AND THE SEA CHEST, OUT OF THE icy water and fell on the bearskin near our fire. Damienne sat beside me, enfolding me in her cloak. My teeth chattered, my whole body shook uncontrollably.

"Monster!" I raged against my heartless uncle with what little strength I had left. "Monstrous to pass us by!"

Damienne's face flooded with tears.

"Murderers!" I screamed at the ships, already beyond hearing.

Damienne clung to me, sobbing. That was all either of us could do. We were so lost—twice abandoned! I realized that Damienne was shivering as much as I. My wet clothes had soaked hers. She began to cough. I had to get us both dry and warm right away. I staggered on my benumbed legs to the sea chest. It had been wrapped in an oilcloth and tied with a rope. I wrestled with the rope, and eventually untied it and unwrapped the chest.

Among Berthe's clothes were many sealed packets. I grabbed two shifts, woolen gowns, and shawls. I helped Damienne strip down and put on the dry clothes. I dressed myself, and we each wrapped ourselves in shawls and cloaks. Our shivering stopped, and feeling returned to my legs. We huddled on the bearskin. Damienne's cough lessened.

"This is Claudine's," said Damienne, fingering the beautiful shawl of dark green and black patterns.

"Did you hear Marie?"

"No."

"They're dead—Berthe, Claudine, Giselle, Antoinette, half of the Maries. Many of the young *sieurs* will have died as well."

Damienne crossed herself. "A cruel waste," she said.

"Aye, cruel."

"They remembered us," she said, and tears filled her eyes again.

"Berthe must have thought of us as she lay dying."

"Have mercy on their souls," said Damienne.

"Amen."

"What else is in the chest?" she asked.

I dragged it close to us, and we began to look through it. Most of the wrapped packets contained food. Every inch of space was packed with food. Dried peas, beans, barley, flour, dried mint, and ship's biscuits were sewn into bags. A small honeycomb was wrapped in waxed parchment next to a packet of dried apple rings. As dear to us as the food were several small, carefully sealed packets of shot and powder. Pierre's friends the sailors must have helped ready these for us. They had packed two shirts and breeches for Pierre.

"This chest is brimming with love," I said.

"And sorrow," said Damienne.

"And sorrow."

We'd eat sparingly of the food, saving most of it. But we needed some of its goodness right away. I needed strength to get us, and the chest, back up to La Maison. We boiled some water in our cook pot, to stew four of the apple rings with a bit of mint and honey, which would ease Damienne's cough. When the apples softened, we ate them in small bites, slowly, carefully, making each mouthful last.

I closed my eyes and tried to remember other apples I'd eaten at times when apples were abundant and common. Pierre and I had climbed into the forbidden trees and pulled apples from the highest branches. We had licked each other's fingers clean. I finished my mouthful of apple, tasting my sweet memory. I opened my eyes to see Damienne with tears streaming down her face.

"My friend," I said, hugging her and wiping her eyes. "Don't weep."

"I am afraid I will die unshriven," she said.

"Dear one, we will be long gone from here, and you will die an old woman in your clean bed, surrounded by your vast family, with the parish priest at your side." I rocked her as I spoke of the fantasy she needed to hear.

"Please God, it will be so," she said. "But..."

She was terribly ill with the white plague, and we both knew the bad air on this island was killing her as surely as the evil mushroom had poisoned Pierre.

"When the natives return with our *canu*, we'll leave here," I said.

"If and when they return, you may not be able to leave," she said, looking at my belly and meaning the babe.

"There's plenty of time before then," I said.

"June," said Damienne. "There is perhaps a month yet when you can safely travel."

"We must only get as far as Saint-Jean's Bay," I said. "The Breton fishermen will help us. The baby will be born there, and then we'll go back to France in the autumn with the Bretons."

Damienne blew her nose and wiped away her tears. "You are right, Marguerite. You see more clearly than I. That is just as the *Bon Dieu* will arrange it."

"*Courage,* my friend."

She nodded. "Now, how shall we get ourselves and this treasure back to our house?"

"Very slowly," I said.

The spring sun released us from the prison of winter. The demons seemed somewhat quelled by spring. At least they no longer howled at night, but every time Damienne coughed I was reminded of their presence. All the snow melted. We bathed in warmth and washed the filth from our clothes and bodies. I aired our rank furs and beat the fleas out of them. We still needed their warmth on cold nights. Pale green spears of onion grass poked through dead leaves, and I chewed them, grateful for the taste of something fresh and green. I planted a small patch of ground near the house with barley and spinach.

Damienne grew weaker every day. I no longer had to order her to rest, because she couldn't as much as walk to the stream unaided. On sunny days I brought her outside to bathe in sunlight. When she didn't cough, she clasped her rosary and murmured prayers.

I tried not to leave her alone too much, but we still needed to eat, needed wood for the fire, and always I was conscious of the time nearing when I'd not be able to fend for us as I did now. Standing, I could no longer see my feet, that big was my belly. Yet I carried the weight of my babe easily, and I'd never felt so strong. I was strong enough to survive my uncle's death sentence. Living would be my revenge.

I roamed the island, setting snares, looking out for the first berries and the first edible greens. I caught fish in the stream and in the gulf. I fed us and replenished our stores. It seemed there would be enough to last us through the time of the babe's birth and some beyond that.

But at every moment throughout each lovely day fear

grew. I fought mine constantly, trying to hope, to pray, to make Damienne well by wishing it with each breath I took. *If she didn't get better... Dear God, if she...* I was afraid to even think the possible horrible end of that sentence. For how could I think of my life without her? I'd survived Pierre's death because of her and his child. But how could I have this baby without her? How could I face each day on this island without her heart to anchor me? How?

Damienne was afraid, too. She feared for her soul, lost for all eternity—although she hadn't spoken of her fear since the day my uncle had sailed past us. Neither did I speak of mine. The unspoken weighed heavily upon us.

April ended. May was sweet with flowers in the open places and violets in the woods. I no longer carried the weight of the babe with ease. I dragged myself from place to place, trying to hunt for us just a few days more before surrendering to rest.

I had hoped that with the coming of spring Damienne would recover. As the days grew longer and milder, I couldn't continue to deceive myself with that hope. Damienne grew sicker and weaker. The balmy days of May passed, and she could no longer hide her fear, nor I mine. We had to speak of this terrible thing.

"Damienne." I summoned enough courage to begin.

"Yes?"

"I am afraid."

"Yes." My friend looked at me, her eyes bright in her gaunt face. "I am, too."

"What can you tell me about having this babe? And what can I do for you?"

"This is all I've thought of for weeks, months," she said, "since the coughing and fevers began. I fear you will have this baby alone."

I wanted to protest and couldn't. We only had time now for honesty.

"I've gone over every moment of Isabeau's birth. I remember it all."

"Tell me."

"When you feel the time is near—"

"How will I know that?"

"There are several signs," she said. "You will have pains, like those of your monthlies."

"I have those now."

"These will differ. They'll grow stronger, and stronger, and come over you like waves, closer and closer together. Your waters will break. It may be a great unmistakable flood or a small trickle."

I would make her tell me these things again. I listened carefully, but my fearful heart got in the way of my hearing.

"You will be restless and fretful."

"I am that now."

"Yes, but this will also be different. Try to heed your body."

"Then what must I do?"

"First untie all things knotted, or cast them out of the house."

"Why?"

"Lest the babe get knotted in its cord."

"Aye. And?"

"Have ready thread to tie the cord and sewing scissors to cut it. Prepare clean linens to swaddle the babe."

"Will I have time to do all this?"

"Yes, there will be time. It's best to move about and be busy, but don't exhaust yourself. You'll need all your strength to push the baby out."

"What if I can't?"

"You can and you will," she said. "Think how much stronger you are now than when you left Montron."

That was little comfort. My body may have grown stronger, but I wasn't sure about my courage. Damienne began to cough. I brought her a broth of mint leaves and honey and waited until she could speak again.

"Now, tell me what I must do for you."

"I need you to help cleanse my heart of sin, to ready me to meet the *Bon Dieu,* that I might live with the angels."

Could I really do all that?

"My head aches with thinking on this," she said. "It may be all right for you to hear my confession and grant me peace in God's name. But what if it isn't?"

It seemed to me that if anyone on this earth had a pure heart, it was Damienne. God would forgive me if I tried to help her in this.

"If it was all right for you to marry Pierre and me, couldn't I do this for you?"

"You are not a Catholic."

I didn't know how to answer that.

"Damienne, we both believe in the *Bon Dieu*. We believe He is just and merciful. The priests might quibble, but He will accept this."

Damienne was silent for a long while. I could see she was struggling with this. It wasn't for me to convince her. She had to embrace it herself to have the peace of mind she needed.

"Ah, Marguerite," she said at last and breathed a great sigh. "It will be so. God will forgive us."

Then she told me all that I must say and do for her. I practiced the words several times until she was satisfied that I knew them. I learned the words and couldn't bear to think of what they meant.

"Amen," she said.

"Amen," I said and let all the tears flow. Now that she could die peacefully, would she leave me that much sooner?

"Promise you will stay as long as possible. There is still a chance."

"No," she said. "There are no more chances. But I promise I won't hurry away from you. I want to see Pierre's son."

She held me in her thin arms as I sobbed.

TWENTY-ONE

～

"I FEEL LIKE A QUEEN," SAID DAMIENNE.

"A queen?"

Damienne was sitting on the bearskin, shrunken in her shabby cloak, looking more like a beggar than a queen.

"Here I am, lying in the warm June sun, and you waiting on me hand and foot."

"At your service, *Vôtre Majesté*," I said, handing her a cup of water and bowing as much as my enormous belly allowed.

"Your service is a novelty for one born to serve," she said, smiling up at me, "but more than your tender care, I feel queenly having all this beauty. Look at that sky, and the clouds making pictures for me," said Damienne. "Isn't it glorious?"

I nodded, watching her face and not the sky. She was more skeleton than girl, yet her face was absolutely glowing.

"How can you be happy?" I asked.

"Because I'm no longer afraid," she said, "not for myself, and not for you."

"But—"

She held up her hand to stop me.

"I *know* this," she said, "as if God had told me directly. You and the babe will be safe. Marguerite, this isn't a hope or a prayer. It is God's truth." Her eyes burned with fever or conviction, or both.

"Think of all that's befallen us. The dark cycle is coming to an end as surely as spring follows winter."

We'd seen enough of the dark soul of the world to last us two lifetimes. I wished that we could now be spared. But Damienne was dying, I'd be left alone, and wishes wouldn't help. I'd not argue with my friend and spoil what little time we had left together. Neither could I believe her.

"I know how you feel about this place," she said. "During the winter I agreed with you, but look around. Isn't this one of God's most beautiful creations?"

I sat down heavily next to her and took her hand in mine. The air was sweet, thick with the feel of life beginning. Across the stream, the meadow grew green and gold, strewn with wildflowers and larking butterflies. Beyond, slender birch and aspen grew light against the dark spruce and pine trees. Birds chirped and squirrels chattered.

"Think how rare this is," Damienne said, whispering now to spare her breath. "In France, only the king has such a forest, and I doubt his is this lovely. The *Bon Dieu* has given us a true Eden. He's shared one of his most beautiful secrets with us alone. I will die a virgin in paradise, and I am content."

I wanted her to fight, to keep living. She squeezed my hand.

"Try to see this as I do," she said.

I sighed and wiped away my tears. As much as I resisted what she said, I couldn't deny the island's beauty. We sat silently. I felt the odd roll of the baby inside me and watched the sunny, playful world. It did seem a small piece of heaven. I might even have enjoyed it if Pierre could have returned from the grave and Damienne could live on.

"Tell me again what I must do when the baby comes," I said.

Damienne told me step by step and made me recite it after her.

"I will tell you as many times as you wish," she said. "Now you must do something hard for me."

"What?" She wasn't dying. No, not now.

"Peace, Marguerite, I'm not leaving you yet," she said. "But soon I must. And you must begin my grave."

"Good Lord, no!"

"Please. It's heavy work. If you try to do it all at once, you'll hurt yourself and bring the baby too soon."

I wanted to cover my ears or run away. Damienne kept on as if she were talking about something as insignificant as when I might start the water boiling for our supper.

"If you start now, and dig a little each day, you can manage it without harm."

"You can't ask this of me."

"I can," she said. "And you will do it, because you must."

That day I began digging a hole for her next to Pierre.

I wept as I worked. Damienne sat on the ground near me and recited prayers and bits of Scripture.

Day followed day. I could no longer hunt in the woods; I was too heavy with the baby. Even had I been able, I couldn't bear to leave Damienne for more than a few minutes each day. I needed to be with her every moment that I could. I caught fish in the stream and snared a few careless rabbits in the meadow. Neither of us ate much. There seemed to be enough stores to last until... In truth, I couldn't look that far ahead.

I watched each day for the return of the natives with our *canu*. But every passing day that they didn't come chipped away at the possibility of risking a voyage to Saint-Jean's. Then, I was too near my time and Damienne too near death to embark on any journey.

Still I continued to watch for the wild men, climbing Mont Blanc every day to scan the horizon. I wanted them to return and feared it, even if we could not travel. Perhaps they would know of some root or herb that would bring life back to Damienne. Hadn't some of their kind given Captain Cartier a cure for the deadly sickness that swelled and blackened the gums?

I watched, but they didn't come.

"Tell Isabeau about what we did here," said Damienne. "Let her know how strong and brave you've been."

"Nonsense."

"Don't you think your sister should know that a girl can learn to shoot a gun, set a snare, build a house, even kill a bear if she has to?"

I didn't. If I could get back to Isabeau, and any normal sort of life in France, I didn't think I would ever speak of this place. Why would I want to remember a nightmare?

"I used to dream about Pierre every night," I said on waking one morning in mid-June. "Now I rarely do. It feels as if I'm losing him all over again."

"Perhaps it is because he is getting ready to be reborn," said Damienne.

"Perhaps." Should the child take the place of the father? It seemed too much of a burden for a milky little babe.

That day I finished digging Damienne's grave. And next to the hole in the ground, I'd gathered many stones to pile on top and protect her from scavengers.

"Thank you," said Damienne.

"*De rien,*" I said and stifled a sob.

"Do me one more kindness."

"Yes?"

"Prepare me to meet the Lord."

"Of course, I will when—"

"Now," she said. "While I can enjoy your touch."

"Oh, Damienne."

"I know this is hard for you."

"Harder than anything."

"Marguerite, my only regret is to leave you alone."

"You did promise not to."

"I did," she said. "And you must forgive me for breaking it."

I heated water and washed her all over. She was as small as a child. I dressed her in Berthe's fine linen and combed out her hair.

"It has grown some, hasn't it?" she asked.

"Aye. It is pretty."

"We three have always been together on this island," she said later as we lay side by side, looking up at the bright, clear blue of heaven. "You and me, and Pierre." She reached out and touched my belly. "Even in the moment we thought we'd lost him, he was coming back to life in you."

I nodded. His seed probably began to grow the very day he died.

"When I am buried," she whispered.

I leaned in close to her to catch her labored words.

"It may seem that I've left you all alone. But you are clever, Marguerite, and may find a way to keep me near. Now, hear my confession."

Her death marched steadily toward us. Damienne seemed ready in her calm heart to meet it. Not me. I rebelled.

"Surely it is too soon. Can you not wait one more day?"

Her eyes met mine.

I took her hand in mine. "Our Father..." I began, barely able to speak for the tears welling up in me. "Thy kingdom come, thy will be done, on earth as it is in heaven."

"Amen."

"Have you any sins against God or man that you wish to confess?"

How could Damienne have anything on her conscience?

"I am guilty"—she spoke with great difficulty—"of envy. I coveted my friend's love."

I squeezed her thin hand. She'd never hurt me with her envy.

"God forgive me if I did wrong in marrying Marguerite and Pierre. It is not their sin, but mine." Her words came slowly, painfully. "And I am breaking my pledge to stay with Marguerite."

At this I choked back a sob.

"Is there anything else?"

"No."

"God forgives you."

"Marguerite, will you forgive me?"

"There is nothing to forgive."

"Please."

"I forgive you," I said.

"Good. Continue."

I said the words she'd taught me, trying to remember that I was to be as a priest, and not my selfish, destitute self. I could at the very least be calm. So I swallowed my tears.

"Do you believe in the ever living Christ? And that His suffering and death were for your salvation?"

"I do."

"Do you give thanks to Him?"

"I do."

"In your sincere belief, and gratitude, in Him, it is as if you partook of his sacred Body and Blood. God bless you, Damienne."

I signed the cross on her forehead. A priest would have anointed her with consecrated oil. Instead, I kissed her and gathered her into my arms.

She smiled, then rested against me. And so we awaited her death.

As night fell she left me with the merest sigh.

"What?" I asked.

And she had gone.

TWENTY-TWO

I KEPT VIGIL ALL THAT NIGHT. COME MORNING, I carried Damienne to her waiting grave and laid her in the cold earth. Then began the awful task of burying her. I knelt by the mound of dirt and pulled and pushed it into the grave, weeping as I covered her. I prayed.

"Hail Mary... Holy Mary, Mother of God, pray for us sinners, now and at the hour of our death." I said it over and over, until it became gibberish, and was the truest prayer I'd ever said. When all the dirt and stones were piled high atop her frail body, I went back into the dark hovel, barred the door, and fell into a long, restless sleep.

I woke drenched in sweat and shaking with fear. I was so alone, so lonely and lost. Awake or asleep, I'd never spent one moment alone at Montron. And since I was six years old, when Damienne first came to live with us, I'd never been without her. Pinpoints of daylight peeked through the walls, but inside was dark and still as midnight. In my sleep the fire had gone out.

Damienne was dead. My grief was as deep and wide as when Maman had died. Only now there was no Damienne, no Pierre, no sweet baby Isabeau to bring me comfort and help me mourn. I was marooned in a wilderness where few Christians had gone before, and none were likely to return. My lonesomeness was vast as the ocean between me and France. And I was faint with hunger.

I hadn't eaten since the morning of Damienne's last day. Hunger moved me from my bed of sorrow and fear to Berthe's sea chest. I crouched there and gnawed at one of the precious sea biscuits, hard and dry as stone. I drank stale water from the cook pot, water I'd last used to bathe Damienne. I chewed and swallowed, pushing away each powerful black thought as it came.

Later, later I will think all the terrible things; now I must only eat.

Once sated, I sat back on my haunches and breathed.

You are clever and may find a way to keep me near, Damienne had said. I certainly wasn't clever enough to resurrect my friend. If I could have done that, I'd have brought Pierre back to us. The babe lurched in my womb, contradicting me. All right, the babe was returning Pierre to me, in a way. But I couldn't be pregnant with Damienne's child, could I?

Damienne had been so full of peace all the last days of her dying. That was what I needed to remember, her peace, not my loneliness.

"Move again, baby. I need your company."

The compliant babe stirred. No longer the little fish aflutter inside me, he was a cramped prisoner of my womb, a solid being waiting to be born. My solace.

And my fear.

Could I bear this child alone? And should we both survive his birth, could I keep us both alive? Was there any point in trying? Death would come with little bidding. Death would be easier.

The baby attempted a somersault. I had no right to deny him life. I would fight for him, if not for myself. My fate was to live on alone without Pierre, without Damienne, and full of sorrow. So be it. I'd make an effort to live. I would feed myself and this child. I couldn't sit weeping by the graves, as much as I wanted to do just that. The babe was coming soon. I had to provide for him, for us. Now.

Thinking thus almost freed me. In accepting the full weight of my grief, I became numb, feeling nothing. Or so I thought. I lumbered to my feet. How simple it had once been to stand up. I collected the harquebus, powder, shot, a sack to carry what food I might catch or find, some dried meat to eat, and a deer's bladder of water to drink.

Should I light the fire? No. There'd be time when I returned. And it would save me a day's worth of firewood.

The day was well advanced, horribly bright and beautiful. I'd ignore its cruel beauty. I kept my eyes on the cracked leather of my boots and headed for the deepest wood.

As I entered the cooler shade of the forest, the mosquitoes

rose to meet me. I didn't bother to swat at them. It would do no good and would simply infuriate me, wasting my strength. Although they pursued me with their incessant buzz and whine, none stung me. So my stench served some purpose. I might have laughed if there'd been any mirth in me. Instead, a sob choked me. I'd thought burying Damienne was the hardest thing I'd ever done. Living without her was harder. And this was only the beginning.

I set several snares, then needed desperately to sit down and rest. I found a big tree to rest against and sank heavily to its roots.

As soon as I was still, the mosquitoes closed in around me. I buried my head in my arms to shut out their noise. And then the voices began. At first it was just the sound of a word or laughter intermingled with the buzzing. Then one voice rose above the buzz and said quite clearly, "Your protectors are dead, Marguerite."

Another whined, "You're all alone."

More joined in to taunt me, "Alone and helpless."

"Stop!" I shouted, looking up and seeing only the insect cloud.

"We'll take your baby!"

"Never!"

"We have you all to ourselves. Nothing can save you."

"I have a gun!" I yelled and struggled to my feet. "I can protect myself."

The demons laughed. Their laughter pursued me as I headed for the clearing.

"There's no escape!"

I ran as best I could, tears blurring my eyes. The demon laughter grew and grew. I felt it ever closer. I had to get away.

"There is no getting away!"

I ran faster, stumbling on roots and underbrush, my breath ragged, my heart about to burst.

My foot caught on a large branch, and I went sprawling, face first, on the hard ground.

At first I could hear nought but my own sobs. As I quieted, the sounds of the wild came to me. Bird song, drone of insects, the barely perceptible rustle of creatures moving all around me. The demons were still. I shakily got to my knees and groaned to standing. I'd fallen full on the babe. I felt my belly over. Had I killed him? No. He moved.

Thank you, Lord.

I picked up the gun and my sack. I hurt all over.

"Enough," I said. "I'll leave you, this day. But I'll be back."

Silence.

I limped back through the woods, across the clearing to the stream. I pulled off my outer clothes and sank into the cold water. It eased my bruised body. I washed away the dirt and my tears. I didn't know if I could go back to the woods. Wouldn't it be handing myself over to the evil ones? Yet game was in the deep woods. I needed meat.

I left the stream and went inside to light a fire. I was not so clever with the flint as Pierre had been. It took me many tries to get a spark and start a flame. Once the fire took, I dragged the cook pot to the stream to fill it with fresh water.

Each simple task was a trial. I hurt from the fall, and a deeper pain throbbed in my back. I checked on the stores to see what remained, to figure how long I might avoid the woods.

Two weeks, maybe more.

I'd go to the shore on the morrow and collect some seaweed, perhaps net a large fish. Not today. There was no more fight left in me this day. I set dried rabbit and some greens in the pot to stew and collapsed on the bed.

"I will not weep," I said. "I will not."

I lay still and tried to pray.

"Hail Mary...Holy Mother..."

A sharp pain took my breath away.

I'd done myself some terrible harm in the woods. Perhaps the demons had already killed me, and it would just take some time to die.

I sat up and a warm flood came out of me. Was it my lifeblood leaving me? No. The flow was clear.

My waters had broken.

Good Lord! The baby was coming!

TWENTY-THREE

***

DON'T PANIC. DAMIENNE SAID THERE WOULD be plenty of time. I didn't care how much or little time I'd have; I was terrified.

Calm yourself, Marguerite. How could I be calm?

We'll take your baby. The demon voices plagued me.

I got up to make sure the door was barred, as if that could protect either the baby or me. I took a deep breath and looked around, knowing that I had to do something, but what?

Loosen all knots. Untie what is tied lest the babe be strangled by the umbilical cord, lest the babe be tied too tightly to me and not get free. I didn't really know why, but I had to do this thing. I walked in frantic circles. Where to begin?

I grabbed the net I'd made for fishing, opened the door, and threw it as far from me as I could. The sunny afternoon stopped me. How could such mildness harbor death or demons? I drew off my wet, sticky shift and stood naked and shameless in the sun. I felt my belly, round and taut as ever. For all the water that had come out of me, the babe was still well cushioned. Perhaps he'd moved lower down, heading toward his destiny and a life apart from me.

I wanted to hold him in my arms, to know that we'd both come through his birth alive. Life was so fragile. Perhaps, inside me, he was the safest he'd ever be. A breeze stirred the air and chilled my heart. I shivered, feeling the danger of standing so exposed in this cruel place.

I hastened back inside. But before barring the door, I took one last look at sun and sky. Perhaps this was the last day I'd see.

I shut the door and began going through all my poor things, untangling all the stubborn knots with shaking hands. I laid out cloths to swaddle the babe and the little shirt I'd made for the baby from one of Berthe's finest shifts. Dying, she had thought of me. *May she be happy in heaven and send her blessings down on me this day.*

Nearly all my loved ones were in heaven, my saints.

"Keep watch over me this day. Pray for me."

"Ow!" A pain caught me unaware. It wasn't a big pain. I shouldn't have cried out. I rubbed my back and walked in a circle. Damienne had said to keep moving, calmly. I breathed. The pain ebbed away.

I opened Berthe's sea chest. Her clothes looked hardly worn, and each garment had been laundered, strewn with fragrant herbs, folded, and carefully put away. Damienne and

I had gone through everything in the sea chest, taking out all the food, and mostly leaving the clothes in their pristine condition. Now, I unfolded each shift, petticoat, and gown, untying pretty silk bows as I found them. All around me lay the beautiful clothes meant to be Berthe's trousseau. My dark shack blossomed like a young woman's boudoir. Inside the last dress, a gown of deep purple silk, I found a flat, heavy parchment packet sealed with red wax and addressed to me. This looked as if it had been purposely hidden there. Damienne and I had left this last gown undisturbed and not noticed the packet at all.

A new pain was coming on. I set the packet down and followed the small circle of my confinement. Whatever was in there would wait.

When I could breathe again without gasping, I folded and put Berthe's clothes away.

I rode the wave of another pain, then broke the seal of the packet. There was a thick, flat cloth square, stitched closed and quilted, and a letter from Berthe.

Ma Chère Marguerite,
Others have spoken against you, not I. I wished I'd had the courage to stand by you, and share your exile.

There are no jewels in Canada and only false gold. We've found savages, murderous cold, sickness, hunger, and death.

Remember me,
Berthe

Poor Berthe. I took out the sewing scissors, snipped the threads on the bag, and ripped it open. Fifteen gold coins fell out onto my bed. Berthe's dowry!

Came another pain, taking me firmly in its grip. It left me sobbing. Berthe had given me so much. The sea chest would help me survive on this island, and should the babe and I leave here, we'd have a small fortune to start a life in France. I began to weep and could not stop. Day slid into night. I walked in circles, wearing a path in the dirt floor. I washed away most of Berthe's sad letter with my tears. By daybreak, the pains started coming so close together, I barely recovered from one when another took its place. I sailed on an ocean of pain and despair. How could I do this by myself?

"Damienne, how could you leave me?"

I looked without seeing or comprehending the dark space that had sheltered us. I lived only in the sensations of my poor body.

"Don't be frightened, Marguerite," Damienne had said. "Think of me, think of the Holy Virgin Mother."

Mary had given birth in a stable. It was probably nicer than this dark hovel. There would have been straw to rest on and cows to comfort her with their hay-sweet breath and large dark eyes. How I'd welcome one of the big golden cows of Montron, chewing her cud beside me.

"Ow!" Pain pulled me this way and that. "Maman! Help me!"

I'd become a giant bloated bug lying on my back, arms

and legs flailing. Mary was never a giant sweating, stinking, naked bug. The pain let go of me, and I lay back panting.

Mary had Joseph with her. She had an old carpenter, not the father of her child. Would he have been a comfort? God was the father—God, the Father. Did she feel Him with her? Could I?

Another pain!

"I can't! *I cannot do this!*"

Again I was lost in the strange land my body had become.

Then something began to happen. I actually felt as if I were opening up to let this baby out. A powerful urge possessed me to push. I grunted and growled, no more Marguerite than the Holy Virgin. I was a beast, pushing the thing inside me out. I had to get it out, get it out . . .

I hit a wall. Neither the baby nor I could go any further.

"God Almighty!"

I writhed and panted, and felt the huge head of the baby pulling me apart but going nowhere.

"Pierre, you monster! Look what you've done to me! *Pierre!*"

I felt such rage that had Pierre miraculously appeared before me, my anger would have killed him. With the rage came greater fear. The babe was stuck. We'd die this way!

"Calm yourself," said Damienne, as loud and clear as my own ravings.

"*Nooo!*" I screamed, and a miracle happened. I felt the baby's head pressing forward, leaving me. Next came his shoulders, arms, and elbows. I felt it all squeezing right out of me. One more wild-animal grunt and push, and the babe came free!

All the mad rage left me. I reached between my legs and pulled my son to my breast. He looked at me with wide, astonished eyes—my baby, my very own. He began to wail, his first cry. All was well; he'd live!

Somehow, I'd done the impossible. I'd given him life. I couldn't rest yet. I had to cut the cord that bound us together and clean my beautiful boy. I looked for the first time at the whole baby and began to laugh. I'd made a girl!

I rocked her in my arms, laughing and crying. The baby settled against me, and her crying ceased. Perhaps I ought to have been disappointed, but I wasn't. This was the happiest moment I'd ever known.

Her perfect little mouth yawned. She looked at me again, the deep round pools of her eyes full of knowing God, ready now to leave God for life with me.

My precious one. My absolute perfection!

TWENTY-FOUR

HER NAME WOULD BE DAMIENNE BERTHE Anne-Marie Pierre. But from the first, I called her Pierrette, my little pebble. I tied the cord two inches from her tummy as Damienne told me, cut it with the sewing scissors, and buried the afterbirth. I drank broth and ate some of the meat I had set cooking the day before.

Pierrette slept, worn out from the struggle to be born, and I dozed beside her.

As soon as I had the strength to walk, I brought her to the stream and christened her. She needed to be in His care as soon as possible.

"I will teach this child, as best I can, to love God and our saints in heaven for whom she is named."

As I dribbled water on her head, she woke, squinting against the sunlight, but didn't cry. I shaded her eyes.

"Yes, little one," I told her. "Now you have a name and belong to God."

She seemed satisfied and returned to slumber.

I stumbled back inside on wobbly legs and barred the door. We slept together on the bed I'd shared with Pierre and then Damienne. I curled around her like a C and dreamed of Pierre. He smiled, sunlight playing on his curls. I felt the warmth of him.

"I thought I'd lost you," I said.

"Never," he answered.

We walked through a springtime orchard. Clouds of white blossoms drifted around us. I held his hand and walked slowly, scattering flowers. A cat mewled in my dream. I woke, startled to find a baby in my arms. My breasts were swollen and hard, full to bursting with milk. Pierrette's mewling cry grew into a loud, pitiful wail; her rosebud mouth transformed into an angry maw.

I brought her to my breast. When she tried to nurse, my milk squirted out, choking her. Already I was a terrible mother. We wailed together.

"Calm down." Damienne's voice came to me, and this time I listened.

I rocked Pierrette and, sniffling, sang one of Maman's songs. Milk ran out of my nipples. Her cry grew less frantic. I grew calmer and sang with pleasure. My tears ended. Her body melted in my arms. I breathed deeply. She found my breast and nursed like a piglet, greedy, contentedly grunting. I was the placid sow, equally content.

She was so beautiful. She reminded me of Isabeau as an infant. I traced the intricate whorls of her ears and the perfection of her tiny fingers. In her, I saw Pierre's pouting lower lip and the dark wings of his brows. What little hair she had twisted into curls, like Pierre's and Damienne's, too.

"Had Damienne lived just two more days, she'd have seen you."

Ripples of emotion crossed her face as she slept. I saw a quizzical look Maman often had, and a frown very like my father's, which made me shiver.

"I will tell you all about the people who've made you, your father first of all," I whispered in her sleeping ear. "I'll tell you about Damienne, Maman, your grandmother, and Isabeau, your baby aunt. She will be more like a sister to you."

I wouldn't tell her about her granite grandfather, nor her great-uncle whose righteousness countenanced murder.

"Your father would have been so enamored of you."

Pierrette smiled and burped.

Oh, Pierre. Holding our child made me long for him more than ever. He had been my rock. Now I had this helpless little pebble, completely dependent on me. Even during Damienne's illness, when I did everything for her, she'd supported me with her faith and love. There was no one I could depend on from this day forward but myself.

"Poor baby, born in the remotest wilderness with so very little of your own."

When Isabeau was born, Maman had ready for her a whole wardrobe of precious little shirts, clouts, and gowns. A few had been mine, but many were newly made for her. And though Father objected, her christening gown was trimmed with frothy lace. I'd pieced together a few shifts and shirts from Berthe's dainty linens. Remembering how quickly Isabeau had grown, I dared not cut too many of the small, newborn clothes. In a short time Pierrette would need more than I could provide from my own rags and Berthe's sea chest. I'd soon be dressing her in rabbit skins.

Pierrette didn't seem at all worried about her wardrobe, or anything else. Waking, sleeping, she seemed content with her memories of God's realm from whence she'd come and her short time on earth. I worried plenty for the two of us. How could I protect her? How could I get us out of this place? If the natives returned with a *canu* for me, could I possibly manage it on my own? Could I convince them to take us to Saint-Jean?

After she nursed a second time and fell into a deep sleep, I went to the stream to wash myself. I was just going to splash myself clean but wound up sinking into the cold water. It flowed over me, washing away the dried sweat, blood, and exhaustion of childbirth.

By the time I got back to her, Pierrette was howling.

I scooped her into my arms and rocked her.

"Hush, my darling. Don't cry. Maman is here."

She calmed down, and looked at me, her eyes wide open. She seemed to measure me with a deep understanding and accept me, with all my faults, as her own.

And I saw her, in that moment, as the babe in my arms and the woman she'd one day become. I would do everything I possibly could to be worthy of her. Oh, my own.

I let myself rest for four days, trying to keep worry at bay. On the fifth I felt strong enough to venture down to the shore, to First Fire. Perhaps I could net some fish or find sea birds' eggs. At least I could gather kelp to fill the cook pot. My stores were low. I had to hunt soon, but the woods frightened me, especially after my last foray, when the demons' threats had been so clear, so terrible. I'd have to bring Pierrette with me, but would that put her in greater danger?

There were so many questions with no answers. I swaddled my child and made a sling for her to ride in, her head resting against my chest. I strapped a sack with the fishing net, food, powder, and shot on my back, and carrying the harquebus, I set out.

A path I'd walked a hundred times before now seemed treacherous, full of tree roots, ready to trip me. I could fall and crush my own child. She and I had come so far, survived so much, couldn't we now just have peace and happiness? Have life?

I made it to the shore without injuring my child or myself. It was a mild summer day. I waded through the cold water, everything around me tranquil. How could I be so afraid in paradise?

I moved slowly against the slight current in the shallows,

careful not to disturb the bottom. Silvery creatures slipped past my legs. I had to be patient and wait for the one fish coming into my net as surely as the one fly that found the spider's web. I could wait. I'd learned that.

It was almost a year ago that we'd been marooned here. We'd had so little and so much to learn about sheltering and feeding ourselves. Already a hunter, Pierre had needed to sharpen his skills, and I had to learn everything. Hunger and cold had taught us.

I'd been clumsy and weak and had grown strong. Not even sorrow could take that away. Perhaps I should teach that to Pierrette, and Isabeau, if ever I saw her again. Sorrow came to every life. Each of us needed strength to meet it.

I felt a tug at the net and pulled up a salmon. I dragged the fighting fish back to shore and threw it up on the rocky beach. If a scavenger came for the fish, I'd shoot it and have more meals.

Pierrette woke up hungry, and I settled on a sandy spot to nurse her. She'd only been on this earth five days, and already she was able to get what she needed. She was teaching me how to care for her. As this island had taught me to be a hunter and fighter, Pierrette would make me into a proper mother.

I caught two more fish, altogether enough food for three days, maybe four. I gathered some seaweed and wrapped the fish in it to keep them fresh. I'd add the seaweed to the cook pot, though I disliked its brackish taste. Food was food. I had to take what I could get. There were still a few hours left of day as I headed back.

Only a little ways inland, the air grew quite still. I noticed the heavy silence first of all. My skin prickled.

"It is nothing," I said loudly to myself. "The absence of wind and the raucous sea birds."

I began to hurry in spite of the weight I carried and my tiredness.

It began with mosquitoes buzzing around us. I pulled the sling up and over Pierrette's head, covering her completely. Still they landed on the cloth, meaning to sting her, the vile creatures.

Buzzing became whispering, incomprehensible at first. I knew what they'd say. I didn't want to hear it. I walked as fast as I could, wanting to get to shelter, to bar the door against danger.

The whispering grew louder. I couldn't not hear it.

"We'll take her."

"No," I said.

"You can't protect her."

"I can. I will."

"We'll have your child."

"*No!*" I raged.

They laughed.

"You will be left with nothing."

"I will kill you!" I screamed.

Louder they laughed.

I brought the gun to my shoulder and fired it into nothing, killing nothing, wasting powder and shot.

Pierrette woke in terror, howling. I patted her, not daring to uncover her. The demons were driving me mad. They would kill me, and Pierrette would be at their mercy. I had to get away from them. I pushed myself faster and faster. My heart pounded, and my breath came ragged and painful. Carrying Pierrette and the fish was too much. Should I drop the fish? No. I—we—needed that food.

The demons closed in on me. I tried to run. Stumbled. Tripped. And caught myself just short of falling. Their laughter grew. I stumbled on.

I shook so much with fear, I was choking. My own fear would kill me as sure as the demons. I couldn't outrun them. I couldn't fight them in any ordinary way. This was the end. The demons would win. They would take my child. I'd die before surrendering her, but that wouldn't be enough. That wouldn't save her. Did I have the strength to...to what? To kill my own child? I stopped in my tracks. I breathed. The demons were bringing me to an impossible thought—the murder of my baby. *No!* I wouldn't be their tool. I dropped the gun and let my mind go blank.

Pierrette wailed.

The demon voices rose.

"Our Father in heaven, hallowed be thy name." I began the prayer I'd said so many times in my life, especially these past months with Damienne. I didn't beg for His help as I so often did but simply spoke the words and left my heart open.

"Thy kingdom come, thy will be done..."

I concentrated on just saying those words of faith and didn't worry that I might not have enough faith in them.

"Forgive us our trespasses as..."

Peace came over me, a peace truly beyond my understanding. I was surrounded by enemies, but fear had left me. Its absence astonished me.

Pierrette still cried. Poor little one; she must have been smothering in the sling. I uncovered her, sat down on a rock, and let her nurse. Perhaps the demon voices continued. I really didn't know. I could not hear them. The mosquitoes remained a nuisance, nothing more.

Something huge had happened, and I hardly knew what. I continued to marvel, to feel no fear, only the subtle pleasure of my baby's nursing. When Pierrette was satisfied, I picked up my burdens and continued, slowly, back to our shack.

I prepared the fish outside by the stream, one to roast on a grill of greenwood above the open fire, the others for the smokehouse. Pierrette slept near me on the bearskin. Her tummy rose and fell in sleep, and her eyelids fluttered, dreaming.

I thought of Damienne, once we'd confronted the fact of her approaching death. She'd been weak and ill, probably in terrible pain that she never admitted, and absolutely fearless.

"'Thy will, not mine,'" she had quoted Lord Jesus.

I understood that now. That's what had saved me. I'd let

God in and given over all my fears to Him. Perhaps I had at last found the faith that had sustained Maman and Damienne.

I would continue to fight to live. I'd do whatever was needful to protect Pierrette and get us away to a safer place. But I would not continue to spend my days and nights in terror. I'd been given this moment of grace. I'd cherish it. I'd leave to the Lord what only He could do. The demons were God's business, not mine. I would work hard, and God willing, Pierrette and I would survive.

TWENTY-FIVE

I COULDN'T SAY THAT THE DEMONS CEASED to plague me. No. Often I was frightened to near hysteria because they were so clever at catching me unawares, and in Pierrette I had so much to lose. As soon as I recognized them, I stopped the frantic rushing of my heart and body. I stood or sat as still as possible and spoke the words of the Lord. I gave the demons to God, as they were His province, and it saved my sanity.

It remained for me to feed, shelter, and protect us from natural dangers. Sometimes I thought I might die of loneliness, but loneliness, I learned, doesn't kill.

Every day I looked for signs of the natives. I didn't scan the gulf for sailing ships because none would come. The king wouldn't send another expedition after my uncle's had failed so miserably. Having nothing else to hope for, I hoped for the natives' return. I sewed a flat quilted pocket that I could tie around my waist, under my clothes, to hide Berthe's coins. I planned how I would pack all that Pierrette and I would require in the two sea chests. I thought out how I'd explain my need to the wild men with words and pictures drawn in the sand.

I worried about their interest in Pierrette. Would they want to take her? I'd die first. These worries brought the demons, always ready to find me in times of weakness or fear.

The natives didn't come.

I carried on with my plan of building a boat. I made models and put them in the stream to see if they floated. Some did, but not when I added a small stone or two. Finally I had a model that seemed seaworthy, and I set out to make it big enough to carry us and one sea chest of provisions.

Pierrette grew fatter and rosier with each passing day. She cooed and smiled readily, delighted in her fingers and toes, and seemed the happiest creature on earth. Flying in the face of what Damienne or Maman would have recommended, I bathed her in the stream or great salty gulf and let her loll about, naked in the sunshine. She browned all over, *ma petite sauvage.*

In fair weather I hunted creatures great and small, gutting, skinning, preserving the meat, and working the skins. In foul weather, I kept Pierrette in *La Maison* and worked on our boat. Fatigue was my constant companion. I exhausted myself caring for Pierrette and trying to provide for us now, and in case the boat failed and we had to last through another winter. My body shrank back to scrawniness—a tough scrawniness. Every ounce of me was filled with pure determination to keep on, to somehow bring Pierrette and myself back to France.

I came out of the dark woods carrying my day's kill, three squirrels and a fat woodchuck. Pierrette slept heavily in her sling. Although upright and walking, I was lost in thought, lost in weariness, more asleep than awake. I came quite near La Maison without seeing them.

"Madame?" What looked like a man stepped out of the shadows. "Madame, can you hear me? Do you speak French?"

I could neither speak nor move. I stood several yards from five rough-looking men.

"We saw the smoke of your fire," said the man, "and came to investigate. We've never seen signs of habitation so far from Saint-Jean."

I stood rooted, staring in shocked amazement.

"Madame, are you well?"

These weren't spirits or demons. They were French-speaking men.

"Saint-Jean?" I said.

"*Mais, oui*, Madame."

"Fishermen?"

"Yes, from Bretagne. We kill the cod and bring it back to France."

I dropped my burdens, and hugging Pierrette, fell to my knees.

"*Bon Dieu!* I am saved."

The men gathered around me, lifted me up, and brought me to La Maison. I still couldn't properly talk, so many tears choked me. Pierrette woke, crying for her supper. I draped her in a shawl to nurse, remembering some shreds of modesty. In feeding her I calmed down enough to tell my tale.

The men promised to take me with them to Saint-Jean and back to France in the fall. I gave them a feast of roasted game and berries.

"You built all this?" asked one.

"My husband, my friend, and I built it all."

"And you survived a winter here, *Mon Dieu!*" said another.

"My husband died before winter, my friend died at the beginning of summer, just before the babe was born."

"Did your husband kill the beast?" he asked, marveling at the bearskin I sat on.

"I did."

"Madame is strong and brave!"

I didn't choose to be either. I had simply wanted to live.

I packed the sea chests with my few things, the Gospel, my ragged clothes, the bearskin, even the deerskin breeches that I would never wear in France. The Bretons helped me collect and pack all the food and skins I'd been hoarding.

"Madame was preparing for another winter," said one of the men.

"Yes."

"Or to sail away," said another, studying my boat. "This is like those *les sauvages* make."

I nodded.

"The wild men came here?"

"Twice," I said.

"And Madame survived!"

And I'd survived.

Pierrette and I went to the two mounded graves to say goodbye. I knelt between them, holding the squirming baby.

"We're leaving," I said as tears fell. "It is all that I've wanted since the day my uncle put us here. And yet…"

We had wrested food and shelter from this hostile land. Here we'd lived our love for each other. The babe wiggled and fussed, impatient and ready to go forward.

Pierre and Damienne were dead, but not the love we'd known. Love could not die. It would travel with me back to France.

All of the fishermen at Saint-Jean treated Pierrette and me with great kindness. They gave us a small shack for our own. They cooked for me, fetched my firewood, and showered Pierrette with attention and presents. I was shy with the men, finding it difficult to be so suddenly among the living. They seemed to know this and left me in peace.

I sewed little dresses and a fine fur wrap for Pierrette's return to France. I pieced together a handsome fur cloak for Isabeau, and one for myself, too. I continued to wear my ragged clothes, saving Berthe's finery for my return. By October, when the men prepared to return to France, I was rested and almost plump.

The winds were with us, and the ocean calm. It was a swift passage back. I worried about Aunt Clemence's reception, but not too much. I had Berthe's gold and some decent clothes. Life might prove hard in France, yet having lived in paradise, I feared nothing.

AUTHOR'S NOTE

MARGUERITE DE LA ROCQUE WAS A TRUE-LIFE heroine. I stumbled upon her harrowing tale while researching the early French explorations of Canada. The most complete account I found in English appears in Francis Parkman's *Pioneers of France in the New World*. His version is based on the *Cosmographie*, written by André Thevet in 1575. Thevet claims to have heard the story directly from Marguerite.

The real Marguerite suffered horribly on the demon isle (now known as Isle de la Demoiselle, in tribute to her). Bitter cold and near starvation weren't as devastating as the loneliness and despair she suffered after the deaths of her unnamed lover and Damienne. Marguerite's painful solitude made her easy prey for the island's evil spirits. The shrieks and taunts of the demons nearly drove her mad. According to Thevet, the only way Marguerite silenced them was by reading aloud from the Gospel.

When the French fishermen discovered Marguerite, she was a wretched stick of a woman in filthy rags, more dead than alive. Yet she had endured in spite of terrible privations, misery, sorrow, and the demons' onslaughts. As Thevet relates, in her struggle to survive she'd killed not one, but three bears, each one "as white as an egg."

A contemporary of Marguerite's, the queen of Navarre, was fascinated by her survival. The queen wrote about it in her collection of tales called *The Heptameron*. The queen altered Marguerite's story significantly, giving her a lawfully wed husband and eliminating Damienne. In the queen's version it is the husband's traitorous act that lands them on the island. Marguerite is the virtuous wife who chooses to share his exile. This is the ending of the queen's tale:

> They [the crew of one of Roberval's ships] took her [Marguerite] with them on their long voyage back to La Rochelle. When the townspeople learned of her trials and steadfastness, she was received with great honor. The ladies sent their daughters to her to learn to read and write. In this worthy manner she earned her livelihood for the rest of her days.

I'd like to think that the queen used her influence to help Marguerite's school for young ladies succeed. After her ordeal, Marguerite certainly deserved a respected and secure position. But I hope that she taught her students more than reading and writing. I hope she told them the true story of her remarkable survival, letting them know that even refined young ladies could persevere and endure.